MISTRESS MOLLY

And Her Senior Sex Club

An Improbable Novel by Sherry Halperin

Cover Caricature by Rachel Druten

Dedication

To all you saucy old ladies out there – BRAVO!

And to my family, I'm NOT Mistress Molly!

Useful Yiddish Words Mistress Molly will say!

Zaftig	A woman having a pleasantly plump body
Yenta	A woman who is a gossip or busybody
Sephardic	Jews descending from Spain, Portugal or North Africa
Balaboosta	A perfect homemaker
Shiva	A period of seven days formal mourning for the dead
Spilkes	Sitting on pins and needles, upset, agitated
Schmear	To smear
Kvetch	To complain all the time
Chazerei	Things of little value, junk
Mezuzah	A small parchment in a container affixed to the doorpost of Jewish homes
Mazel	Good luck
Chanuka	Festival of Lights holiday in Jewish families, celebrates freedom from oppression
Farklempt	Unable to speak, choked up
Oy Vey	Oh no! Display frustration, grief, dismay
Nosh	To snack

Contents

PROLOGUE

"Hey, Mistress Molly. You have a visitor."

The guard at the police station unlocked my holding cell and escorted me through the dark hallway into a stone cold, window-less room furnished with a single gray steel table and two metal chairs. I immediately noticed a dank smell which was at first hard to identify. As the heavy door closed behind me, the stank hit me again and I surmised it was either an accumulation of recent farts or stale tobacco breath. I have the nose of a perfumer and a vivid memory of both fragrant farts and cigars.

As the police person's strong arm guided me to one of the hard seats, the skinny, mustached man continued in his gravelly voice speaking directly to the forty- something year-old man standing next to the table. "Is this your Mama?"

The visitor's body was still except for the slight left to right movement of his head, noting disbelief. He fidgeted with the papers he was holding and finally spoke in a calm voice. "Ma, what the hell were you thinking?

Chapter One

My Past:

Papa, I'll work in the store so sis can go to summer camp.

Mama, I'll stop my piano lessons. I know they're expensive.

Sam, I'll finish college after you, my darling. Get your degree and get established. We've only been married one year.

Not to worry, darling. I'm strong. I'll beat cancer.

Not to worry, dear. I'm strong. Sam was such a good man.

It's true. You blink and decades pass. You struggle, you compromise, you go without and for what? They say it's a blessing to do unto others. But when does it become time to do unto yourself? Selfish? No, truthful but not always possible.

It's almost over. The years tell me so and my wrinkles and brown age spots don't lie. The aches are my battle songs and my metal hip, a badge of honor for the years of housecleaning, carpooling, grocery shopping, working in the office and taking care of the tribe. Most of the time, I loved being a mother, wife, lover and I always tried to put the family first. Sometimes, I resented it. Now, the family is grown and I'm no one's wife or lover. Time has caught up and I've become a tired old lady. Doesn't that sound depressing? Well, it's true.

And yet, in the wee hours of the morning between taking a pee and grabbing a slice of chocolate pudding pie, my over active mind still fantasizes of what still could be. Of who I could be. My curious organ of a brain that has experienced love, sadness, joy, complacency, fury, keeps screaming like an Italian giving birth in a Fellini movie. *Get up you old fart and do something exciting before the last chapter ends. Don't do it for your kid or grandkid. Don't do it because it's right. Do it because it makes you happy, Molly Shapiro. Eat the whole damn pie, swim in the pool naked, order the most expensive dinner on the menu. It's finally time, Molly. It's time to do whatever "it" is. If not now, when? MOLLY SHAPIRO, IT'S YOUR TURN!*

Chapter Two

My Present:

Two Bam!

Three Crack!

One Dragon!

I was winning royally. Mahjongg on Wednesday afternoon with Sophie, Bernadette and Peta was a staple. The game location changed but not its veracity. We're competitive, fierce players. We're four elderly broads with way too much time on our hands. Mahjongg, Dominoes, Bunco – each had a weekly day dedicated for play. Monday, Wednesday and Friday from 11 AM until 4 PM, lunch and a glass of wine included.

Three more moves and I took the four-dollar pot. "Girls, you need to challenge me. It's like taking candy from . . ."

"We know, Molly," Bernie interrupted, "Like candy from a baby. You're so predictable."

Yes, predictable. That's me and my three best friends. We were all widowed or divorced ...single Yentas passing time together as we wait to pass away. Depressing and yet true. Our ages - between seventy and seventy-six. Our lives, as mundane as white bread.

It wasn't always that way.

Bernadette: the youngest, platinum blond thanks to Miss Clairol, five feet nine, skinny, narrow shoulders and huge fake breasts, thanks to Dr. Slevinsky. She modeled until age twenty-three when she met her husband while competing in a Miss New Jersey competition. Five children later, her hopes for ever modeling again disappeared. She was an overly dedicated mother who quietly resented every minute of Cub Scouts, soccer games and homeroom bake sales. She often said her husband sabotaged her birth control pills just to keep her knocked up and fat. Her favorite chatting topic: "I could have been a super model if only . . ." Although we don't consider Bernie a true alcoholic, she does enjoy a five o'clock cocktail no matter what time it happens to be. She and husband, Mack, traveled to California twenty-five years ago for the job opportunity they hoped would change their lives. Too bad Emu never caught on as a chicken substitute.

Widowed for fifteen years, two of her sons died in the same car accident that killed her drunk husband. Her surviving children remain in New Jersey and never come West for visits. No wonder she imbibes on a daily basis.

Peta: the exotic one, red haired, thanks to Nutrisse, still with a wowzah body minus minimally drooping boobs and tush, tall, Marilyn Monroe mole on her right cheek. She came to Los Angeles from London in her late twenties after a failed marriage and worked as an exotic dancer at one of those places near the airport. I think it was called Bottoms Up. Between her sexy British accent and bombshell body, she had no problem meeting men and marrying three more times. Sadly, they all died. Investigated after each demise, all were deemed to be by natural causes. Who knows! We don't ask. Last funeral was seven years ago. No children.

Sophie: average height, brown hair, ethnic large nose, a bit chubby, full lips and zaftig. She thinks her life was very similar to mine. She married her college sweetheart, had one child who tragically died in infancy of a mysterious flu, inherited a boat load of money when her film producer father passed away and divorced her husband when he lost her fortune and went to jail for fraud. To this day she defends him for selling six hundred percent of a film's possible value – thirteen times. Sophie is rather naïve. Divorced for ten years, Sol died in prison a few years ago, finally admitting to his criminal activities.

Me: average everything, except my big brown eyes and jaguar paced mind. I'm fortunate that my grey hair is soft silver rather than steely white and my complexion is naturally bronze. That comes from the Sephardic side of my family. Now that I think of it, I'm nothing like Sophie. I didn't inherit gobs of money when Sam died. He left me just enough to pay off our little house. He never went to jail or had anything to do with show business. He was a CPA. I never finished college and my one and only marriage was arranged by Sam's and my parents. Traditional as my life has been, it's been predictable and it did give me a brilliant, handsome, successful son. A balaboosta, I'm not. I've been widowed for eight years.

The four amigos. As different as our pasts, we share a similar present.

"Molly, another piece of coffee cake?" Today's game was at Bernie's Sherman Oaks apartment. The hostess added, "How about another Arnold Palmer or some decaf? I can spike the tea."

"Not now, Bern. Stomach is off."

On that refusal of food and drink, the group's chatter came to an abrupt halt. Looks went from one friend to another, with nods of silent understanding that something must be very wrong for me not to eat. You need to understand that food, gossip, playing table games and general complaining was our air, our sustenance, with food highest on our emotional barometer.

None of us work. Not because we don't want to. Who hires a seventy-year-old when a perfectly capable thirty-year-old wants the job? We do a little charity work for Meals On Wheels, collect Social Security, but mostly play games and complain. Of the group, I am the fortunate one with my son only ten miles away. His name is Stanley, the lawyer. I see him and his wife Hilda and grandson Ben once a week for Sunday dinner. I cook, they eat, we do the dishes and they leave.

The other girls rent. I own a small cottage on Valley Vista, a nice street North of Ventura Boulevard in Sherman Oaks, California. Sam and I bought it in 1977. It's old, needs new everything but it's been my home for over forty years. My son was raised there. Sam started his business in the spare bedroom shortly after we moved in and I sat shiva there when he died.

We all shop sales, only eat out at Early Bird dinners and search Groupon for deals. This is the existence of septuagenarians on a very tight budget.

Bernie filled my half empty glass with lemonade tea, even though I said I didn't want any more. She then sat at the game table and started the inquisition. "So, dish. What's going on, Mol? Spill." She amazingly still had that sharp New Jersey accent.

Sophie wasn't one to let some gossip go by and quickly chimed in, "Is it your son? Is he getting a divorce? Shame."

"No." I blurted loudly and spit three times over my shoulder to ward off that evil possibility.

Then Peta added her two cents. "Leave Molly alone. She'll dish when she's ready. But I bet I know what's got her panties in a bunch. That retired insurance salesman you went out with two weeks ago, the one from Match. You found out he's married, right Mol? Told you something was fishy."

All my friends were wrong. There wasn't a specific thing that was getting to me. It was an accumulation of weeks, no months, of frustration and apathy that led to my current major case of the blahs.

"Are you all happy?" I finally asked.

"What's happy?" Peta answered, shrugging her shoulders as she popped a mini bagel in her mouth and adjusted her bra straps.

"Happy. Content. Fulfilled." I got up and walked to the window that overlooked a Target parking lot. "I keep thinking that there has to be more than

Wednesday Mahjongg and Inter-faith chair yoga at St. Margaret's on Thursday."

"You don't like our game?" Bernie asked a little annoyed. "Maybe we should take a break from Wednesday and play on Monday. We could play Bunko on Wednesday and Mexican Train Dominoes on Friday. Would that be better, Molly?"

I chuckled to myself at Bernie's ridiculous reasoning. They didn't get it. I needed a complete break from static routines, from the lack of excitement in my life. "Bernie, it's much more than the day we play Maj. I'm seventy-two years old. I have arthritic knees, a pacemaker and thinning hair. The highlight of my day is the fact that I wake up. And my kid and his family – they love me, but don't ask. They have their own lives."

The group nodded in unison. "My kids are almost strangers." Peta added. "I'm lucky if I see them once every five years."

"At least you have family." Sophie added.

Molly continued. "I have shpilkes. That's what I have. I pace around my house. I can't stop thinking of what my life could have been – what I could have done if I followed my dreams instead of Sam's. We all did that in the sixties and seventies. It was more than compromising. It was bending to other's wishes without regard to our own. I want to be excited about something when I get up in the morning and not because I've had a successful BM." The girls laughed.

"Are we too old for a new beginning?" I asked.

Then Bernie asked the million-dollar question. "Mol, so what is it you want to do? What were, or are your dreams?"

I paused. "I have no blessed idea. I remember wanting to be a veterinarian at one point. And, of course, I wanted to be Debbie Reynolds or Audrey

Hepburn." I swallowed hard, realizing these memories stirred up lots of feelings. "All I do know is that I need to change something before I wind up in a place for psycho seniors. People look at me as if I'm finished with life. I hate that. I want them to see a vibrant woman who has possibilities."

I had obviously struck a major chord with my friends. Bernie looked away and started to softly sniffle. Sophie fidgeted with her napkin and Peta crossed over to the hall mirror and pulled back her jowls trying to create a younger looking face.

"Me, too." Peta finally said in her low, sexy voice, walking back to the table. "I used to be a vivacious, sensual woman. Now I'm embarrassed to strip in front of my doctor. You could land a plane on my ass and sweep the floor with my tits."

And with that, Bernie and Sophie admitted they were stuck in the old lady rut as well. It was unanimous. We all wanted change.

"Bernie, I'll have that cake now," I announced.

With a mouth full of Entemann's from the day-old bakery, I continued. "So now what? We'll buy a yacht and sail around the world?" The girls agreed that would be nice. And then Peta added that the yacht had to come with a hair dresser and cook.

Sophie added her two cents. "Yeah, a yacht on our budgets? More like a plastic raft from the dollar store."

I nodded and took another gulp of my Arnold Palmer. "Let's meet at my place tomorrow for lunch? I know it's not our regular day but consider this an emergency session. I'll make a pasta casserole and a cake. Got coupons. Come up with ideas of what we can do to spice up our lives. Be realistic. Not pie in the sky when I win the lottery ones."

And then looking seriously at my three friends, I spoke like I was channeling a wise clergy at a church service. "Change is scary, but being stagnant could be our death." I took a cleansing breath realizing the depth of my statement and continued. "Sophie, shmear a bagel for me. Suddenly, I'm ravenously hungry."

Chapter Three

All the way home I questioned what I had just put out into the ether. Stagnation and complacency were the de rigueur du jour in my circle of friends. We accepted what we had been dealt. Oh, I'm not saying we didn't whine. That action took up about sixty percent of our lives. We kvetched, grumbled and complained about everything from the cost of health insurance to the lack of eligible men to date who could get an erection. And in the end, we stayed the same. But now, I had this bug in me – this inexplicable voice that kept chanting *If Not Now, When*? Was it a premonition of my death or was it the realization that I was still alive? Whichever, it was strong, undeniable and something I needed to understand.

I passed the 24-Hour Gym on Ventura Blvd. and vowed to exercise more. And then I drove through a McDonald's and got a vanilla ice cream cone from the dollar menu. My life had been one of many paradoxes. Strong but compliant, with an intelligence that was kept hidden to make my husband emperor of the household. That's what we did. If we weren't a pot smoking hippy back in the day, we were a *Leave It to Beaver* wife. In case you don't know, that was a television show that depicted the perfect, white family with a strong father, subservient wife and a mischievous child.

My house literally had a picket fence. The second drawer beneath the electric stove was full of aprons and pot holders. My Teflon coated ironing board, the one I used to flatten pillow cases and boxer shorts, proved I was unmistakably of the Beaver generation. Women's lib has passed me by and the traditions of my parents painted the life I had led.

Bernie helped clear the table. I poured another cup of coffee for Peta. The elephant in the room had to be addressed. I sat and softly spoke. "So, I've been thinking. Actually, I was up most of the night and have decided that I'm going to put my house on the market. I've refinanced twice but still have some equity in it."

The girls just stared at me. I expected at least some gasps or an *Oh My* in disbelief. Nothing. "As I was saying, I think I want to sell my home, move and I also think you all should come with me." The quiet was unsettling. "Well, speak, old ladies. Don't just sit there like dried up prunes. What do you think?"

Peta was first. "Are you fucking kidding me?" Somehow saying fuck with a British accent sounded conventionally acceptable. "Where the hell would we go? We have our lives here."

"What lives?" I asked.

Everyone had a reason to stay put from car insurance paid for the year, to knowing the neighborhood, to not wanting to pack up an entire apartment. Bernie said she had signed up for a Senior Zumba class at the Y and couldn't go anyplace until the class was over. Sophie complained that finding new doctors would be way too hard.

"That's ridiculous." I said and continued. "We need to look at the broad picture. Where could we go that the cost of living would be lower, has lots of social activities to offer, good climate and welcomes seniors with open arms? Somewhere with little or no ageism."

Peta raised her hand like she was in grammar school. "Ou ou ou, I know, I know. Newport Beach. It's beautiful there."

Sophie answered with, "And one of the most expensive places in the world to live. How about Florida? No state tax, low cost of living, warm weather.

21

Miami or Boca or Sarasota. Lots of old people there. I hear there's a great circus training place in Sarasota."

"So, you want to run away to the circus?" I chimed in. "What would you do, be shot out of a canon or ride an elephant? Anyway, Florida is too humid and I think that circus school shut down. I hate bugs. More ideas. Where else?"

For the next twenty minutes we thought about what states, towns, countries would be perfect. From New York to Texas to Costa Rica, we dismissed each location as too cold, too rural, too expensive or too far away.

Then Bernie came up with the idea that would change our lives forever. "How about the place that never sleeps, the place where there's still shrimp cocktails for $2.99 and buffets on every corner? The place where dreams come true and fortunes are made."

Bernie was being very dramatic. "And where we could live around the corner from Mr. Wayne Newton."

Las Vegas sounded just perfect.

Chapter Four

My house sold in two days. The market was sizzling and I got a few thousand over asking. It must have been a sign that I was doing the right thing.

Peta, Bernie and Sophie gave written notices to their landlords and started to clean out closets. There were a lot of details to work out. As planned, I would buy the house in Las Vegas and the others would help by giving me monthly rent payments in an amount that would be probably less than they were paying in Los Angeles. Their share would help with the mortgage payments, utilities, taxes and food. Basically, our arrangement was like me being the dorm Mother and the other girls the residents. We talked about signing an agreement but figured it was useless. We all were bonded at the hip and would never hurt the others. Words for some to live by, until they aren't.

We used my driveway for a huge garage sale and raised over two-thousand six-hundred dollars to help with moving costs. You should have seen the chazerai we sold. From Peta's Queen Elizabeth dolls to Sophie's movie posters to my collection of Lladro porcelain animals, we cashed in on the stuff that was stored away in boxes marked 1990.

Meanwhile, my son was furious. "What the hell are you doing?" he kept asking. My answer was always the same. "Starting a new life."

"You're leaving your family, your grandson, for what, a whimsy, a senior crisis? See a shrink. Get counseling. Go on a cruise. You need money? I'll give you an allowance." Stanley just didn't understand. I didn't want my son's money. I wanted new adventures.

"Sweetie," I replied, "remember when you wanted to raise a pig on the 4 H farm? You were nine years old. I told you it wasn't a good idea because eventually it would be sold for bacon."

"Yes, Ma, I remember," Stanley replied. "But after months of begging, you did buy me a piglet. Remember, I named him Morrie, after Uncle Morris."

I walked over to my son and rubbed his back. "And Stanley, what happened when Morrie was a year old and weighed 250 pounds from all the good food you fed him?" Stan tilted his head as to say he had fed the animal well and what of it? I continued, "You cried and said you should have never gotten the pig. Well, this move is like your pig. We may only have a few years left to stuff our mouths and role in the mud, but we're going to have fun doing it no matter how much you or anyone else objects. But not to worry, sweetie, we won't be slaughtered. The opposite, we're taking this deep dive to survive."

"I don't understand the analogy," Stanley said, shaking his head in disbelief.

"Either do I, my darling. But it sounded good, didn't it?"

We made two trips to Las Vegas so Shanna, the realtor we found online, could show us around. We viewed homes from the North to the South, Henderson to Summerlin and finally chose one in a gated senior community. It offered everything from pool aerobics to bocce ball to knitting classes. There were three club houses, tennis courts, putting greens, an eighteen-hole golf course, indoor pools, outdoor pools, gyms and restaurants. The house had four bedrooms, an open kitchen/living room concept with a small pool in the low maintenance desert landscaped back yard. Fifteen minutes from the strip and eight minutes from a hospital, the latter a very important factor for us septuagenarians. It was unanimous that the beige stucco house that looked like ten thousand other beige houses in Senior Lakes was the best value for our, or should I say my money. The name of the community gave me a chuckle since there were no lakes within fifty miles but the idea of having over fifteen thousand old people looking for a life beyond retirement was certainly appealing.

We were so excited. "Oh my god," Peta screamed. "This is going to be our home. Maybe I can get a job in one of the hotels shows? I still can kick a mean can-can and my voice still can carry a tune."

"Sweetheart," Sophie answered, "They'd hire you only if the revue was a spoof on over the hill strippers."

"You're mean, Sophie," Peta replied. "But I guess that's true."

We all laughed as we drove along the Strip and looked in childish wonderment at what would soon be our back yard.

Chapter Five

The house was empty and my emotions raw. Compulsive person that I am, I swept, vacuumed and dusted every inch of the place making sure the new owners knew it had been well taken care of.

So many events. So many memories - a long loving marriage, a child, successes, broken bones, birthday parties, illnesses. There were more happy moments than not which caused me to second guess this huge decision I had made. But I came to the realization that the memories were cemented inside me and the house just a shell without my Sam. I chanted to myself, *be strong,* as I stroked the front door mezuzah left behind for good luck. The young couple who bought the house should only have the mazel I did.

The moving van pulled up to each of our homes exactly three months after our momentous decision. There were tears as I hugged my grandson and whispered in his ear. "Nana will only be a four-hour drive away. And you can always call me on your cell." I couldn't believe Stanley had given a nine-year-old an iPhone. My old flip was still working just fine. I didn't understand my Stanley and he certainly didn't understand me. But a deep love was still there. "Ma," Stanley said in a stern lawyer like voice, "if you need anything, let us know. I still think this move is nuts, but it's your life. Just be safe and careful and ,,,," And with a kiss on the cheek and a tear in his eye, my son was gone, leaving me as I left him years ago at his college dorm.

Peta and I drove in my six-year-old tan Buick. Sophie took Bernie in her 2004 black Mercedes. Both cars were piled high with art, computers and other items we deemed too valuable to ship with Mayflower. The four of us would share the two cars. No need for additional insurances.

Two pee stops, a taco stand burrito, a photo op at the world's largest thermometer and we were in *the city of a million secrets*. Mayflower pulled up a half hour later and the move-in began. "That goes to my room," I ordered. "Be careful, that dresser is an antique." The moving guy gave me a strange look as if to say "like you, old lady."

Peta and I had done a mock floor plan and knew where each piece of our collaborative furnishings would go. "Sir, would you move that couch a little to the left?" I asked politely. "Yes, that's perfect." We shifted, lifted until we couldn't.

It was the middle of October and the evening was pleasantly cool. If I had to guess, I'd say it was about seventy-two degrees. We took a moment to sit by the pool and recoup but by 7 PM, we were all ready to put that saying of being in a city that never sleeps aside. Totally spent, I dozed off fully dressed on top of my unmade bed.

I remember day one in our new home so well.

Woke up to the wonderful aroma of freshly brewed coffee. Sophie had been up for almost an hour and was totally taking charge of the kitchen. She had emptied the coolers we brought from California and filled the refrigerator with essentials. "You want scrambled or sunny side up?" she asked overly cheery.

"No eggs, just coffee, "I answered in a somewhat robotic voice. I wasn't used to having someone cater to my morning needs. I actually wasn't used to having another human around before noon, period.

One by one my roommates appeared, blurry eyed and achy. The awe of the move had been replaced by the realization that we still had a ton of work before we could say we were settled in.

"My back is killing me." Bernie complained.

"Stop kvetching," I blurted, "You're the youngest. Suck it up. In two more days, we'll look back and just laugh that we thought the move was hard."

Well, five days later, with the help of Advil, Ben Gay and heating pads, we finally got things to a state where we could see the floor and counter tops. Dishes, pots and pans were in their cupboards, books on the built-in living room shelves. Thank goodness Peta is tall and Sophie strong. The two of them measured, hammered and hung fourteen pictures to perfection. Bernie arranged the linen closet and broke down all the cardboard boxes. I dusted and vacuumed as each room was complete.

We were done. We were home.

Chapter Six

O ur first month in Las Vegas was manic. We visited the Club Houses every day and signed up for exercise classes, yoga, pool aerobics and games – lots of games. Monday was canasta, Tuesday we played Bunko, Wednesday was Dominoes and Friday, Mahjongg. It's hard to give up old habits. Anyway, the surroundings were new and there were fresh faces giving us welcoming smiles. Then there was Peta who winked at every person with a penis.

We visited one mall after another as well as every hotel and casino. Our favorite was Caesar's followed by The Venetian. Oh, and then there were the shops at Paris and Wynn. We loved them all.

About four weeks into our new adventure, I was cooking a Shepherd's Pie as Bernie set the table. "You know," I said, "during our first month, we've spent way over our budget. At this rate, they'll be nothing left for emergencies."

"What are you saying, Molly?" Sophie asked as she poured a glass of Two Buck Chuck Trader Joe's white wine that now was over three dollars. "Are we in trouble already? It's only been a few weeks."

"A little over a month," I corrected. "I wouldn't say trouble but it sure would be great if we could make some extra cash. Otherwise, we really will need to cut back on eating out, even at the early birds." I was more than just a little concerned. I had already supplemented our kitty to keep finances on track. Yes, I had a bit more monthly income than the others but surely not enough to support four people in a city that bursts with temptations.

"I think we need a meeting.' I said as I slid the pie onto the oven's bottom shelf. "Peta and Sophie should be back from shuffle board any minute. Bernie, think about ways we could make some extra cash and we'll get ideas from the other girls, too. After all, we're resourceful women on an adventure."

We switched our wine to merlot and ate the Shepherd's pie, mostly in unusual silence. It was evident no one had any ideas of how to supplement our income. We didn't in California and nothing seemed to be different in Nevada. Peta finally suggested we give dancing lessons in our living room. "They have classes at Clubhouse Two," I noted. "And they're free." Bernie chimed in.

Everything suggested was either being taught or needed too much capitol to start. Knitting classes, Mahjongg classes, flower arranging, aerobics, all offered at the clubhouses at Senior Lakes. Bernie continued,

"That's why people, actually us, why we moved here. It has everything."

And so, it did. At Senior Lakes one could play golf in the morning and learn how to change the oil in your car at three in the afternoon. Book Clubs, Play Reading Clubs, Tarot Card Clubs were all available.

"I know what they don't have," I offered enthusiastically, "They don't have an affordable bakery for homemade cookies and bread and cupcakes. We could start cooking, put up notes on the clubhouse bulletin boards and sell from our kitchen. Everyone loves home baked stuff, especially the men. What do you think?"

Peta got up and went to her recipe box on the kitchen counter. "I can do my banana bread and pumpkin bread."

Then Sophie added, "And my cheesecake is to die for. I can make those individual ones with graham cracker crust. Right? What can you bake, Molly?"

"Well," I answered, "I've been known to make some pretty darn good cupcakes for my grandson. And chocolate chip cookies with nuts are my specialty."

All of us shared what we could contribute except Bernie. Apparently, she had never done much in the kitchen and baking was definitely not in her wheel house. So, Bernie became our PR person, designing flyers and posting them all around our huge community. She also was the cashier and helped package the baked goods.

Seemed like a great idea. We baked, we boxed, we advertised, we sold. Only problem was that we didn't do the math. At the end of our first few weeks, we were three-hundred-eighty-seven dollars in the hole. Chocolate and nuts were expensive and so were the fancy little containers we chose to package our gooey delights. Business geniuses we weren't. And the ten pounds we each gained quality tasting our products didn't help our morale. Our baking idea was put in the garbage.

"I'm serious, ladies," I was preaching to my roomies while gently jogging in our pool, praying the cookie pounds would magically disappear. "If we don't get some revenue in, we're going to have to sell the house. I tried to budget but we're spending considerably more than we have and I can't keep coming up with the difference. I'm thinking the move was not a good idea. I'm so sorry."

We had settled into our new lifestyle and my message of trouble was difficult for all of us to stomach. Peta was making lots of friends, mostly male. Bernie was smiling more than I had ever seen. She started taking cooking classes in Clubhouse three and was learning how to crochet. And Sophie, she had become queen of the drama club. Me? I was still looking for my passion. My periodic alarmist tirades regarding our financial woes were taken seriously, for about an hour and then it was back to playing slots, eating out and splurging on non-essential home decorations.

It had been three months since our move. I had spearheaded this adventure and the responsibility I felt made me more depressed and frustrated than ever. I went back to Sherman Oaks during Ben's December holiday break and celebrated Chanukah with the family. It was a nice visit but I was eager to get back to the girls. Once home, my Stanley called or texted me almost daily asking how things were. He sensed that life wasn't as flawless as I had hoped. I mostly lied and said "Perfect, darling. Couldn't be happier." But inside doubts were mounting and I wondered how long my charade could go on. We absolutely needed to either cut our living expenses, get outside jobs or win big at a casino. The change was good. The pressure I had mounted on myself was bad. My head was playing a looping tape and I didn't know how to shut it off. Same old problem with no one coming up with a solution.

Chapter Seven

I t was mid-January when we took a very propitious drive. Rather than be tempted to shop or go to a casino, we decided to explore the outskirts of Las Vegas. Our route headed us West and then North West along U S 160. There was sand everywhere and very few homes or stores. Some think desert landscape is beautiful. We all agreed it was depressing.

About an hour into our little car trip, Peta announced that she needed a bathroom. Sophie chimed in that she had seen a sign about a mile back for a place that sold eggs. "They must have bathrooms there. Get off here, on Reservation Road and head back," she suggested.

The building looked like a country store with roosters and chickens painted on the clapboard and pictures of lovely ladies across the front.

"This doesn't look very much like a market but the sign did say Chicken Ranch," I said, "Let's see if we can use their facilities. We'll buy a dozen eggs as a thank you."

The four of us stood in the entry way, mouths agape and just stared. There were pictures of beautiful women, half naked, all over the walls. The smell of perfume mixed with tobacco filled the hallway. It was dimly lit. No counter for the sale of eggs. No chickens for sale.

"Howdy Gals, I'm Belle. What can I do for you charming lassies?" A buxom lady in her mid-fifties came out from behind a red velvet curtain that divided the entry and an adjacent sitting room. Belle was as formidable in appearance as sweet in tone. Tall, hardy, she looked like a wrestler in the throes of transitioning. "You know we don't have gentlemen here." She chuckled and continued, "Oh we have plenty of men but none for sale, if you know what I mean. I'd try Chap's Paradise about four miles down the highway. They have a good selection of really cute boys."

Sophie was the first to speak. "Ahhhh, Miss Belle, we stopped to buy some eggs and use your facilities . . . bathroom facilities. Thought you were a country food ranch."

Peta blurted out, "Where the hell are we? This place looks like a whore house."

Belle corrected. "A brothel, Missy. A very upscale, legit, hugely successful place to service the needs of men." Peta backed up apologetically bowing.

We forgot that we had to pee. None of us had ever been exposed to anything like this. Well, Peta had been an exotic dancer back in the day but only took money for her dancing. She swore that sex was off the table in her clubs. We didn't believe her.

I looked around the room dressed in burgundy velvet couches and Tiffany style lamps and finally spoke wondering if anyone could see the light that just went on in my head. "Belle," I cleared my throat. "We're actually doing a column for a senior newsletter back in

Vegas and would love to be shown around. Sorry for the ruse about having to pee. Didn't know if you'd let us in. But now that we're here, could we use the bathroom and take a look at what you offer, your prices and ask a few questions?"

Belle smiled and answered, "Of course, ladies. Any PR is dollars in our garters. You live in one of those planned communities? Lots of fellas there, right?"

I winked at the others as we followed Belle down a long hall with pictures of more beautiful, exotic looking women. I had something up my sleeve and the girls immediately caught on.

"Belle," I said, "You're right. Lots of fellas and I bet tons would love to read all about you and your gals. What's the average age of your customers?"

The questions came flying out of me like a vending machine plied with quarters:

"What do your girls make on a daily basis?"

"What STD's do you have to be concerned about?"

Bernie secretly started recording Belle's answers on her smart phone. I continued.

"Do you take charge cards?"

"Are most of your customers locals or men just passing through?"

"How do they select their lady?"

"Do you ever get older gentlemen in here?"

Belle was candid and handed us a menu of services offered. I put it in my pocket. We chatted for at least twenty minutes and her business seemed to be running like a Fortune Five Hundred. She showed us her Nevada license, shared how the state had legalized brothels in 1971 and said that there were currently twenty-one in operation. After thanking our hostess and promising to send her a copy of the fictitious article we were never writing for the non-existent magazine, we got in the car and headed home.

The ride back was relatively quiet. Peta asked, "We know you have something up your sleeve, old lady. Do you want to share?"

"Not yet," I answered and kept driving through the dust of the desert toward the early evening lights of the Strip. I was contemplating an idea that was so obscure and random that I was afraid to say it out loud. It didn't make sense and yet, it was positively logical.

I pulled up at Four Queens and announced that their early bird was open until 7 PM. Over a slab of $7.99 prime rib au jus with sides of mashed potatoes and onion rings, I cautiously started to reveal the concept I was hatching.

"Now, this is just a seed of an idea. It may sound bizarre or well, actually illegal, at first, but hear me out." All four of us had our elbows on the table leaning in so I could whisper. I didn't want to be heard by anyone passing by or at an adjoining table.

I continued. "We all agree that money is needed. Right?" The girls nodded in unison. "And what we learned at the Chicken Ranch is that there's a definite clientele of needy men willing to pay for us."

"What do you mean us?" Sophie asked.

"Women, Sophie, us women." Bernie said in a tone revealing she was annoyed.

The idea of offering sexual favors in our senior retirement community was conceived that very day. It would be discreet, by invitation only, cash and if anyone spilled to management, we would deny it passionately and declare the informant mentally diminished, a diagnosis easy to establish in a community where the average age is approaching eighty.

And so was born our Senior Sex Club.

Chapter Eight

For me, the entire purpose of this journey was to spice up my life. Remember, I was bored and wanted to strike out and accomplish earth-shattering achievements that would show my family, friends and primarily myself that I was more than a stay at home, boring housewife. The reality of having spent an unfulfilled life was depressing and enigmatic. I had what so many wanted – a loving husband, enough money to own a modest home filled with modern conveniences and clothing bought at main stream mall department stores. My son was an honor student and overall good kid, my parents lived into their early eighties and I became the go-to person when any charity needed a worker. A do-gooder. Reliable Molly Shapiro. What I didn't have was self-esteem. I wasn't

Miss Popular or Home Coming Queen in high school and no creative talents. My ego was always pushed aside to massage those around me. That's what I was taught. That's what I did. This club, the business that I would develop and run, would be my deliverance from the mundane. I just knew it.

There were so many questions to be answered. I guess it's that way with any start up. But this company had special complications. I knew what I wanted to do could be construed as illegal. Alright, basically, it was illegal. Money for sexual favors. I kept asking myself what constituted sex. And would it be a sexual favor if no one paid specifically for it? I had no intentions of getting a business permit or license. Everything would be done on the down low. I think that's how the kids explain nefarious actions these days.

On the positive side, I truly believed the club would help people, like a charity with cuddles and kisses as the reward. The income would support my roommates by enabling them to stay in a house and community they were loving. It would help the hundreds, if not thousands, of Senior Lakes widowers and lonely men who thought their days of physical connection were over. Physical contact is so important. I Googled and read every article I could find on the correlation of body connection and the longevity of life and discovered that it's an undisputed fact that even the simple act of hugging prolongs life. The club would be a life-saver.

I went so far as to daydream that my business would someday merit some honor of distinction for saving the lives and sanity of mankind. Or, at least it could bring much needed and deserved happiness in my little corner of the world. I had to convince myself that Senior Sex Club was a positive and needed enterprise.

My roomies were skeptical. Truth be told, none of us had participated in coitus for many years and really had lost almost all interest in it. Dates consisted of some petting reminiscent of tenth grade and lots of kissing. Of course, we all were postmenopausal so pregnancy was no longer a worry, joking we were probably virgins again and that our lady parts were full of dust and cob webs. That said, intercourse was off the table.

I took out the menu that Miss Belle had given us and made copies for Peta, Bernie and Sophie. "No way," Bernie shouted over breakfast the next morning. "I'm not doing that, or that, and absolutely not that." I chimed in that the menu was just suggestions. We could limit or expand on whichever choices we desired. Like we could have a room just for cuddling. "I'm up for that." Sophie volunteered.

Peta was the bravest and said she would do anything above the waist. After all, she had danced topless for years. Bernie said she would watch some soft porn to get ideas but her Catholic upbringing would definitely limit her activities. "When's the last time you were in church, Bernie?" Peta asked. We all knew the answer to that was many, many years, if not decades ago.

Within a few hours we put our menu together, discussing the pros and cons of each act. Taking into account the age of our prospective clients, how long could we give for each performance? Twenty-minute hand jobs would be $25. We would need to buy lots of lotion. Fifteen minutes of cuddling would be $20. Make out sessions with only above the waist feels would be $25 and dry humping would be the Cadillac of the club at $50 with a session lasting thirty minutes, happy ending or not. The activities were a communal decision,

all agreeing that intercourse was definitely off limits –
at least for now.

I had visions of walkers lined up the length of
our sidewalk, bowls with packets of Viagra for purchase
in our living room, mainly for the men's erection egos
and a nurse on call in case of an emergency. Each of
our bedrooms would be used for customers with me, the
self -appointed Mistress, managing traffic and money.
My biggest worry was how to make sure the secret of
our homegrown brothel was kept mum. Maybe a
confidentiality agreement between client and business
would be necessary. It crossed my mind that my Stanley
could draw one up in a few minutes. Nonsense, I
thought. He must never know. As far as he's
concerned, we were still in the baking business.

Chapter Nine

L ife for my roommates continued routinely as I privately created a business plan. I don't think they believed I was serious since the subject was not brought up once during the next week. No discussion. No questions about the menu we had worked on or anything else. It was like the idea never existed. I knew they were leery of my brothel enterprise. That's right, I'm calling it what it is. I knew I had to come up with something to entice them into accepting the concept, to show them the possibilities of having fun while giving others pleasure. I had to get them totally onboard.

"Grab your purses, ladies," I announced one evening about two weeks after my initial proposal, "we're going to the strip." There was never any argument when I suggested a visit to downtown or one of the hotels. But this excursion would be different, kind of a preschool for prospective ladies of the night. Bless the Internet. I had done my research and found several clubs that I thought would give us a taste of how it felt to be seduced and possibly aroused, sensations none of us had experienced for a very long time. If we recognized the sense of someone lusting after our body, it would be much easier to do the same for others.

"It's late, Molly," Bernie said. "Almost time to watch a rerun of Big Bang Theory."

"Not to worry," I answered, "You can catch the same rerun tomorrow. And if we're lucky, we'll get a big bang from where we're going."

As we piled in the car Peta insisted on knowing if she was dressed appropriately. Sophie answered that Peta dressed seductively whether we were going to a lecture on arthritis or an early bird dinner at Treasure Island.

"Don't you have anything to wear that covers more of your breasts?" Sophie continued. "And those pants, they look like they were painted on."

Peta snapped back, "You are just jealous. I still have curves. You look like Sponge Bob's sister."

I had to jump in and quiet the women. No time for arguments or insulting jabs. We were on our way to school.

"OK, Mol, where are we going?" Bernie insisted about three minutes into the drive.

"We're going to Hunk Heaven, a male strip club. I researched them all, Crazy Pants, Hunk Oasis, Kings of the Strip and chose this particular club because it advertises *that women of all ages*, which includes us, will enjoy the entertainment. Any complaints?" Since I didn't get any back talk, I gathered all were amicable to our outing.

Only Peta had a comment. "Oh, this is going to bring back so many memories. Wonder if the place will have poles like we did." I wanted to say that their poles were the significant body part on each entertainer but decided that was too trashy and too soon. My seductive mind had surfaced after being dormant most of my life.

The outside of the building looked like almost all the other strip bars with neon flashing lights in the shape of cocktail glasses and a huge Hunk Heaven sign brightly inviting in customers via a line of moving arrows pointing toward the entry door. There were posters of well endowed, eight packed, oiled skinned men displayed behind glass cases with their names boldly exhibited. I guess once inside the establishment you could request a visit with Ricky, Cowboy, Terminator or Sledge.

Inside, music blared with a bass so loud that it vibrated the windows. Only a few lights lit the place and they were just neon stripes on the ceiling. I nudged Peta and pointed at the stage announcing, "See, they have poles. Feel at home?" She didn't answer but gave me a "I told you so" look.

A lovely bare chested male host escorted us to a bank of seats about five rows back from where the action was taking place. Peta quickly reached into her purse and squished a twenty into the young man's pant belt. He immediately ushered us to the front row and informed us of the two-drink minimum.

"And what can I start you beautiful ladies off with?" inquired another young shirtless man. He was probably in his early twenties and a senior at the University of Nevada. He continued with an adorable, enthusiastic smile that encouraged a huge tip. "Our specialty drink tonight is Sunflower Suprise, vodka and orange juice and ...." Sophie interrupted and asked "Isn't that just a Screwdriver?" The waiter smiled, nodded and said "Exactly, madam." He rattled off the other specials and we all ordered Pina Coladas that were served with little umbrellas and a cherry on top.

One hunk after the other graced the stage, all with chiseled physiques and bulges in the right places. They shook, gyrated, thrusted and maneuvered their bodies like I had never seen. I wasn't totally naïve but Sam and I were, how can I say this, quiet in the bedroom. There were never games and the missionary position was basically all I knew. Looking at these Adonises made me wonder what sex would be like with no inhibitions. I was mesmerized with how they moved their bodies and the sexual innuendos all the gyrations implied. I felt my blood stirring up feelings that had been long dormant between my very puritan legs.

At first Sophie kept looking away but eventually took her hands down from covering her eyes and smiled like it was Christmas. Bernie was clapping, hooting and thoroughly enjoying herself. And then there was Peta. She kept reaching out to the stage trying to grab a dancer's leg when suddenly, one blond dude grabbed her hand and pulled her onto the stage. She was ecstatic and joined the boys with bumps, grinds and several pole spins. She remembered it all. The few ladies in the audience screamed with enthusiasm egging our friend on to the point of her slowly unbuttoning her blouse and throwing it to us. There was Peta, seventy-four years old, gyrating half naked on a Las Vegas stage. She was in heaven and I knew I had enrolled my roommates in my Club.

We experienced the private room, with Terminator and Sledge, had a lap dance, with each of us consuming the mandatory second drink. We left completely exhausted, a little tipsy, smelling of musk and very, very happy.

Chapter Ten

With the girls onboard, I could move forward at a faster pace. Protecting ourselves from the Senior Lakes management and the law was necessary. We decided a membership to the club was paramount. It would establish a clique, a brotherhood, if you will. An initial fee of fifty dollars would be collected from each man entitling the holder to a laminated membership card, free bubbly or flat water upon entrance at each visit and a five minutes use of an onsite computer where said member could watch porn prior to their specific session. I scoured non-disclosure, confidentiality agreements online and came up with the following:

This agreement is entered in to on the ___day of _____, 2022 between the private enterprise of Mistress Molly's Senior Sex Club, hereafter known as MMSSC and _____ and that the activities and actions of the club will not be disclosed to anyone outside Club members. Failure to adhere to this agreement will automatically necessitate expulsion and disclosure to next of kin, clergy and/or employer if applicable. By signing this contract, you agree to the sanctity of this arrangement and promise to hold the ethics of the club to the highest standards. It is understood that this is a Club that you are joining of free will and that any activity entered into while visiting is an act between adult friends and mutually consented upon.

Signed by: Molly Shapiro, CEO of MMSSC

Signed by: _____Member of MMSSC

Sophie had adequate talent on the computer and came up with several designs for business cards thanks to online formats. They had to be two sided with a burner cell phone number on one and seductive boudoir pictures of us on the other. Which brings me to the photo session.

Boudoir pictures for elderly ladies. There were no listings on Yelp or Google for photographers specializing in scantily dressed old ladies. But I did find a man who specialized in photo manipulation. "Yes, Lew, I'd like to set up a session for the four of us. We're in our seventies and want to look sexy. You heard me right. Old. Sexy. Now, can you do that? You must have lots of those fancy camera filters." I was direct. Lew was very convincing of his talents and a session was set for next week. Meanwhile, we all went on a strict diet, laid by the pool to get tan and caked on mounds of Olay Regenerist Anti-Aging cream hoping it would take off at least thirty years.

Lew's studio was a warehouse about a mile off the strip in one of those industrial areas that housed things like flooring showrooms and stores that sold professional restaurant pots and pans. All four of us had hit thrift shops during the past week and brought a suitcase full of sexy night gowns, baby dolls and silk pajamas. "Geez," Bern exclaimed shortly after arriving. "This place is so cold my tits are at attention on their own." Sophie added that she thought her sexiest outfit ever was just a man's pajama top. I agreed and while Lew set up lights, I ran out to Main Street Thrift and bought a pair of light blue men's cotton pajamas. "You can keep the bottoms," I told the young salesgirl. She didn't even blink.

Judy, the makeup and hair artist Lew had hired, worked her magic on us while he did the finishing touches on the set. There was a four-poster bed prominently placed on a raised platform with fake walls on three sides creating the illusion of a boudoir. The bed was dressed in pale pink lace linens. An adorable smiling Teddy Bear graced the pillows and a painting of three nude cherubs frolicking in a meadow was centered on the wall behind the four-poster.

"Who's first?" Lew asked. Peta, who had some modeling experience during her pole dancing days volunteered. Bernie, who if you remember had done quite a bit of modeling in her youth, said she would go second.

"What kind of music do you ladies like?" Lew continued.

I said classical.

Peta said Broadway.

Sophie said seventies rock.

And Bernie said she preferred no music so she could hear Lew's instructions. Bernie's hearing was questionable.

Barry White blasted through the speakers.

Flashes went off, poses taken. Stiff and timid at first, everyone started to relax with Lew's encouragement. "Kneel on the bed and pretend to be a wild cat," Lew instructed. When it was Peta's turn, she cuddled the Teddy Bear placing a hand prominently on its crotch giving Lew a leering smile. Sophie laid on her stomach and seductively ate a popsicle. Then Lew suggested we do a two-some shot, so Bernie and Peta kneeled doggie style looking at each other with their faces almost touching. The girls alternated in front of the camera so no one got too tired and in four hours,

Lew felt he had gotten what he needed. We didn't tell him what the pictures were going to be used for. Actually, we told him that we each had boy friends and these shots were going to be surprise Valentine Day gifts. He assured us they would be seductive but in good taste.

Secretly, I wanted them to be a little naughty. That's why I put on that pajama top and did a few shots for Lew while the others packed up and put our props in the car. After all, Judy had already done my makeup and hair and a teased updo should never go to waste.

Chapter Eleven

"**N**ana, is very busy, sweetheart. I'll call you back tonight." My grandson, Ben, wanted to share that his pet tarantula had escaped and his mother was freaking out. "I'm sure you'll find it," I told him calmly. "Meanwhile, give Mom one of her special cans of tea, the one marked Arnold Palmer Spiked."

I put down the phone and went back to looking at the proofs Lew had sent over. They were good albeit quite fuzzy, purposely to hide wrinkles. But, the idea of what we were offering certainly was obvious. I actually liked the fact that our faces were not in focus. Mystery is everything when it comes to sex. Each of us chose our favorites. Just as Sophie was about to scan them into the mockup business card, I got cold feet and decided that the pictures made our venture too blatant, too obvious and could get us into immediate trouble. Instead, we just used the cell phone number in bold letters and Social Club on the back. Off to Kinkos for two hundred and fifty cards. The photos, well they will be kept for a boyfriend gift if any of us ever gets one.

I wanted to apologize to my roomies about the two hundred-fifty dollars I spent on the boudoir pictures but figured we could put them in frames and use as a sales pitch once a possible client was in our house. Or, we could just save them for affirmation of our womanhood in case any of us doubted our venture.

Besides, it was a fun day for all.

We were almost ready to open. All that was needed was a nurse, Viagra to sell, a case of water, printed versions of our menu and several bottles of hand sanitizer. We each spruced up our bedrooms, adding candles and scented botanical flowers in pretty little dishes on our night stands. Family pictures would be placed in dressers during business hours.

Bernie volunteered to take a free CPR class at one of the clubhouses which we rationalized would be as good as a nurse. At least she would know how to revive someone if he had a heart attack while getting a hand job, thus enabling one task to be crossed off our list. We had our membership cards laminated at a cheap printing place off of Las Vegas Blvd. since Kinkos was too expensive and bought the water and hand cleanser at Trader Joe's. Now all that was needed were the blue pills.

"I'm going to Mexico, ladies, to get our men some ammunition. Anyone want to join me?" I asked.

"Si, senorita," Peta answered. "My Spanish will come in handy. Where we going? Los Algodones?"

"No," I answered and added that Los Algodones is famous for its' dentists and we needed pharmacies. "TJ, Tijuana." Both were about a five-hour drive. I suggested if we left very early the next morning, we could do a turn around and save by not having to stay overnight in a motel.

One afternoon of planning, six-hours of sleep and a very long ride, we crossed the Mexican border and drove the last sketchy mile into town. My research showed that if we bought Viagra in quantity, we could get it for as little as a dollar each. Maybe less. Compared to buying it in the States, that was almost a four- dollar savings per pill. If we packaged them separately with a price of three dollars, we would be making a three hundred percent profit on each sale. And, every customer would be saving twenty-five percent and not have to face judgement at his local Walgreens. I liked my math and rationalization even though I wasn't sure the percentages were correct.

Never occurred to me that by selling the pill we would be committing another illegal act or that since we weren't offering intercourse on the menu, the blue pill really wasn't necessary. Actually, the pill became another income source. What they do with their erection after they leave is their business.

"Il Farmacia?" Peta asked holding her stomach like she had the trots. The sweet woman pointed us to a string of store fronts half a block away.

The sales person behind the cash register of the first place quoted us three hundred and thirty-two American dollars. I did some quick division and figured they were charging a dollar twenty-five for each pill. Il Farmacia number two, a couple of doors down the block, was a little cheaper. We hit gold at number three, a place called Farmacia a Las Estrellas.

"Lady," the man in a white doctor's jacket said in perfect English, "If you buy a very large quantity, I can get the price down to two hundred and twenty dollars."

"Look," I said firmly, my feet digging into the cement floor, "I'll give you two hundred dollars cash and you'll divide the pills into packets of twenty-five each. Deal?"

"No!" He said emphatically, as if I had insulted his mother, sister and the scroungy dog lying in the corner licking its privates.

"Your choice," I replied as I gathered the girls and walked out. We didn't take more than fifty steps and he came running. "Ok, OK, OK" he screamed as he almost tripped on the sidewalk. "You wore me down."

The deal was set. Packets were stashed in our back packs, purses, bras and between the folds of the two Mexican blankets we bought to show customs that we did purchase souvenirs. We had enough Viagra to serve a fleet of jaunty men with age related ED.

On the long ride home, there was time to really discuss how we each felt about the new business.

Sophie: "What do I have to lose? I have no family. If this business will bring in the kind of bucks you think it will, I'm totally for it. I don't like being poor. It's bad enough being old. Look, I haven't had male contact in a very long time. I'd actually pay the clients instead of them paying me for some hugs and a feel. Ha! If only my father was alive. He'd make this adventure into a blockbuster movie. Wonder who he would star? I would pick Bette Midler."

Bernie: "I'm alright with everything as long as my kids back in Jersey don't find out. Who am I kidding? They don't give a damn about what I do. Ya know, I once thought I would rule the runway. I had cheek bones envied by Brinkley and Tarlington. My waist was twenty-two inches and my breasts saluted on their own. Anyway, if there's a chance this will be the adventure of my life, bring it on. I did watch that X-rated Behind The Green Door movie on cable. Paid almost fifteen bucks. I'm certainly not as talented as Miss Marilyn Chambers but boy, some of it looked, how can I say, challenging. Been practicing on a banana. Gotta get my technique down."

Peta: "Well, this is just a hop, skip and jump from my pole dancing days. It will be fun getting back into the seduction game. You know, that's all stripping and exotic dancing is – seduction. Of course, I'm much more reserved and bashful now, so you can understand my slight hesitancy."

We all said in unison, "You, bashful?" And then had a good laugh.

Me: "I had never strayed during my marriage. To say that I'm a Madame of a Brothel is certainly a mouthful and a sharp left turn from how I've lived my life. Maybe I should just refer to myself as President of the Club. But I'm proud to have come up with the idea. We're going to make gobs of money, my friends. I know it. I'm quite farklempt that you all trust me. That means so much. And just think, this coming summer we'll probably be able to get out of the sweltering heat of Vegas and go on a Mediterranean cruise. Maybe Princess or Celebrity. And if this cockamamie idea is the avenue of how we can finance our lives, I'm in with all my heart."

Home at last. Contraband secured. Feeling invigorated. Tomorrow, we open.

Chapter Twelve

I called a meeting right after breakfast. Strategy needed to be discussed. Today Peta would be visiting different community clubhouses and discretely handing out our business cards. She was instructed to only give them to men we knew were not married and those who had hit on her in the past. That was probably at least ten percent of Senior Lakes. If someone called the cell phone and showed interest in joining our club, he would be instructed to come to the house at a specific time, given the location (our address didn't appear on the card) and bring cash for initiation. My job would be to take care of having the confidentiality agreements signed and collecting the initiation fees.

"Now girls," I was deliberately being very professional, "there are new statistics out that will definitely help our sales pitch once the prospective client is at the house. Listen up. I heard this on Good Morning America, or was it The Today Show? Anyway, it was this morning. We'll inform the client that men who do not have regular sexual release die on average six years earlier than those who do. Also, it's proven that loneliness takes off a good three years. With those stats I'll close the sale by asking which of our menu selections they would like and how many blue pills, if any. They need to know that happy endings are not guaranteed."

"Got it," Peta replied and continued, "I have to admit I'm a bit nervous. What do I say if a guy asks what this is all about when I hand him a card?"

I answered, "We're a gentleman's club. Or just say we are interested in meeting men in our community.

That's honest. We just got to wrangle them here. If you get tongue tied or don't know what to say, just excuse yourself and call me. Go check your bedrooms, ladies, they may be getting used in a few hours."

Peta left for the clubhouses and the rest of us sat around nervously watching The Price Is Right and Judge Judy. My heart was beating like I had just climbed three flights of stairs. I was so jittery that Sophie had to tell me three times to stop using the television clicker to check the time.

It must have been two hours before Peta got back with the news that she hadn't handed out one card and didn't know if she ever could.

"I froze," she said, "I just flirted my normal way, got a few men's attention and then ran into the bathroom and threw up breakfast. That was in Clubhouse Two. Then I went to the pool hall and the same thing. Bloody hell, I don't know what came over me."

"Not to worry, dear," I encouraged, secretly feeling my blood drain and momentarily going light headed. "I'll go with you tomorrow. It'll be fine. Let's forget about business today, take a dip in the pool, swim some laps and get rid of all this stress."

If Peta froze, I wondered how any of us could do the necessary marketing. She was definitely the most outgoing and free spirited of the group. Was I completely questioning the feasibility of our project? I had spent a good seven hundred dollars on the pills, gas to Mexico, business cards and the photographer. If we decided the club was not viable, then what next?

I had failed at so many things in my life. I'd start something, like learning French, and stop when I couldn't trill my r's. I failed at knitting, getting my real estate license and becoming an antique appraiser.

Wanting a success, the yearning to accomplish, longing to be recognized was stronger now than last summer when all this began. So why did I question? Maybe it was because we seniors aren't taken seriously and that we are often looked at with pity. Our ideas are constantly put down therefore our egos get diminished. So many of us have accepted the conventional reality that by being old you have to give up on a positive, exciting life. I didn't want to be one of those people.

These thoughts just made my desire to achieve stronger. I've mostly been a more cup half full than empty gal and I definitely have never taken the easy way out. Well, maybe the time I bought store made brownies for Stanley's fourth grade class picnic. But lots of Moms who weren't bakers did that.

"Peta," I said as we did feather kicks and arm swirls in the pool, "I have an idea how procuring clients could be much easier. Let me think about it a little more and we'll talk tomorrow. Kick away and firm up those gams. Olive Garden for dinner, ladies?"

Chapter Thirteen

The delicious smell of dark roast coffee woke me up at eight. Sophie had baked corn muffins and Bernie was watering the patio plants. "Where's Peta," I asked half awake and sipping my caffeine fix.

"She was gone when I got up an hour ago." Bernie offered. "I have no idea where she went. One of the cars is gone."

There was a small man-made lake near Clubhouse Three that Peta frequented. She loved feeding the ducks and had shared that it was her serenity escape. Sure enough, when I pulled into the parking lot, I saw her sitting on the grass with a bag of bread, feeding the friendly feathered critters.

"So, you're running away?" I asked walking over to my roommate and sitting on the ground next to her.

"Not exactly running. Just look at that clear sky. You can see all the way to heaven." She answered.

"You know you'll be paying the cleaning bill if I get grass stains on these slacks. Want to talk?" I inquired as I squatted near my friend.

Peta has always been the most interesting of the four of us in my humble opinion. Between the lilting British accent, which she had managed to keep while living in the States for forty odd years, and the mystique of all her husbands' deaths, there was never a question of her ability to charm men and women. Her spitfire wit could win over the most negative dowager. I was eager to know what was going on in that redhead's mind so I continued to probe. "Come on, Peta – spill."

"Molly," Peta was talking in a quiet, almost child-like tone instead of her normal husky voice. "This whole sex club thing is bringing up reminders of my strip club years. It was a different time. I was a different person. I did things then that I'm not proud of."

"I thought you said you were just a dancer and loved it?' I asked.

"Yeah, a bare breasted performer who gyrated against a pole with men leering at me like I was a fruit to be picked up and devoured. What was there to love? When I think about that period of my life, I feel embarrassed. Am I going to feel that way about this business? If so, I don't want to do it."

I reminded Peta that it was at the strip club she met husband number two, and eventually, number three and had met some lovely women whom she admired.

So, everything about it wasn't horrible. There had to be something else bothering her.

"Molly, have you looked in a mirror undressed lately?" Peta fed another duck and then turned toward me and continued. "I have and I don't like what I see. So how on earth will a man be attracted to my body? And you're right, I did meet Oscar and Jake at the club and they brought me some love and financial security. But I was very proud of the way I looked back then and actually felt pretty great about what I was doing."

That was it. Body image insecurity. I reminded Peta that compared to all of us, she was the one who men lusted after and was drawn to like a piece of crisp bacon. Bottom line, I surmised, was that she didn't want to be seen naked.

"Totally understand, Peta," I said trying to console. "But just think who your clients will be. I personally don't know any man between sixty-five and eighty whose six pack hasn't turned into rice pudding. More than half of these guys are overweight and the other half have balls that drag on the ground. If we talk about my new marketing plan it may calm your worries."

To unburden the image of selling sex, I proposed that we just refer to our organization as a club for dating. Instead of collecting fees for services, we'll have a donation box with suggested amounts. We'll still have the confidentiality agreement signed but with a lighthearted flare that joining the club will be like belonging to a secret exclusive society. "Peta," I continued, "think of it as a fraternity for old folks. I know you never went to college, but believe me, much more went on behind those frat house and sorority doors than what will be happening behind ours."

Peta limberly got up, stretched out her hand and helped me up from the grass, followed by a huge hug.

"A dating club," she said. "I can live with that. But please, Molly, can we get blackout shades for the windows? I'm talking ink black shades so smell, sound and touch are the only senses working."

Two days later, the shades were installed. It was time for Peta and me to approach prospective clients. Since the weather had turned a chilly sixty degrees, I wore casual jeans and a blouse with the top three buttons undone. Peta dressed in tight pink knit slacks, a low-cut orange vee-neck sweater and three-inch heels. I wore my blue tennis shoes. The coffee hut in Clubhouse Three was packed with men who had just finished their morning golf. After surveying the group who were wearing the worse golf clothes imaginable, we ordered two lattes and approached a man we knew as Pete. I'll just be using first names as not to get anyone in trouble.

"How are you? Nice seeing you. How was your game today?" Pete was delighted that Peta had talked to him. She continued. "Join us for coffee?"

The seventy-six-year-old widower excused himself from his buddies and sat down at our small table. After some small talk about the weather, his golf score, the Homeowners Association election and the stock market, I started to tell him about his chance to be a founding member of a very exclusive organization.

"We just feel that at our age, it's hard to find companionship? Do you agree?" I asked. After he did, I added, "So, Pete, would you like to come over to the house and talk about this some more? Peta will be there, of course, as well as our other roommates. We'll be serving wine and pastries. What do you say?"

After he gladly accepted, I gave him our address, my card with the phone number on it and told him to show up at four this afternoon.

We then went to Clubhouse Two, spotted Glenn and basically did the same routine. Another Clubhouse, the pool hall and gym, netted us four prospective clients, all scheduled to show up in three hours.

It was our grand opening day. We had selected the men carefully, all needy, all single, all healthy looking. The question unanswered was whether they had any interest in physical contact. How stupid I told myself. They're men and they're alive. And then I remembered the one thing I had forgotten to buy in case a gentleman had an unexpected happy ending. Condoms!

Chapter Fourteen

Having never purchased prophylactics when married, I was baffled by the huge selection at Walgreens. Thank goodness Peta was there to advise. I hadn't realized they came in colors, sizes, designs, ribbed, extra ribbed and super reservoir. With three boxes of very straight forward Trojans in hand, we found the K-Y lubricant jelly across the aisle and bought a few tubes.

"Why do we need condoms if we're not having intercourse?" Peta asked. I answered that I didn't want to mess up our pretty sheets with a man ejaculating all over them. We keep our clothes on – well, at least most of our clothes, but they can strip down to whatever they like. After my friend stopped laughing, we put two of the boxes back, kept one just because and found some cheap towels to use with the K-Y for hand jobs. My sexual inexperience was showing. I was the mastermind of this ingenious business and I absolutely didn't care what the cashier thought when checking out. I'll never forget the smirk on his face. The checker boy couldn't have been more than twenty years old. I handed him the Trojans, K-Y and towels as he starred at us in what was either disbelief or disgust. "Yes," I said to him, "Old ladies have sex and trust me, it's wonderful." Of course, I didn't know if it's wonderful or not since it had been so many years since I had participated in that activity.

As it inched closer to four o'clock, I grew more nervous. The pastries were displayed on a lovely red serving tray thanks to Sophie. Tea and coffee were ready to serve. Trader Joe's Two Buck Chuck (still over three dollars a bottle) was poured in a cut glass decanter.

Pete arrived ten minutes early, followed by the others. We schmoozed, snacked, and finally, it was time for me to give the pitch.

"Gentlemen," I cleared my throat. "Welcome to the first meeting of our very private club. Let me tell you a little about what we are planning. But first, since it's so very exclusive, I need you to sign these confidentiality agreements."

Glenn seemed uncomfortable at first but after seeing the other men laugh and sign the paper, he put his Hancock on the line. "As you all know," I continued, "closeness, companionship and yes, sex, is vital to our longevity. So, MMSSC is dedicated to resolving all those problems, specifically for elderly, single men and those with wives too ill or unwilling to perform. Basically, we're a health club." I explained that we're not prostitutes – far from it. We're single business ladies who enjoy the company of men and who enjoy giving their men unexpected pleasures while enhancing their life expectancy. "So, who would like to see our menu of delights?" All four raised their hands simultaneously. I had piqued their interest. This was good. "But before anyone gets to experience today's free samples of what's to come, you need to pay your initiation fee."

Bernie and Sophie collected fifty dollars in cash from all except Pete who only had forty dollars on him. He promised to pay us the rest later that night.

"Gentlemen, here are your choices." I announced as Sophie handed out the laminated cards.

There were exclamations from all, from holy shit, to count me in. "So, you're opening a whore house?" Glenn exclaimed.

"No!" I was a bit annoyed and then explained to Glenn that he was free to go if he thought this was that kind of organization. I also reminded him that he had signed the agreement. "There will be no ill feelings if any of you would like to leave. Feel free."

"Not a chance," a man named Sam barked back. "I've dreamed of this day since I was fifteen.

Sophie took Glenn by the hand and headed back to her bedroom.

I took Pete.

Peta wrangled Sam, the pool hall dude, down the hall while Bernie left with the seventy-five-year-old weight lifter and coyly went back to her private sanctuary for their ten minutes of heaven.

In what seemed like a moment in time, we all came back to the living room. Each of the fellows had huge grins on their faces as they high fived each other. Appointments for future visits were entered in my date book. Glenn made two. I handed out cards as each left and told them to be very discreet who they gave them to or the business would vanish. They promised.

Over pasta and turkey meatballs, we debriefed.

Sophie: "It was awkward at first. We laid down on the bed and before I knew it, he had his arms around me, and his tongue down my throat. While walking down the hallway, I informed him that it was just going to be cuddling and kissing and he seemed fine with that. I was okay, but happy when the timer went off. Sure, my lips will be chapped by tomorrow."

Peta: "Once in the bedroom I slowly started to unbutton my blouse, like I did at the strip club. But before I knew it, the dude was helping me unfasten my bra and tossed it across the room. We kissed, nibbled and motor-boated for the entire time. It was actually fun, with his face between my boobs making sounds like an outboard engine. Surprisingly, I wasn't embarrassed."

Bernie: "Well, the research I did really paid off. Once I told him that I would happily give him a blow job, he had his pants off in seconds. No erection but the licks, flicks and ball kisses really turned him on. He definitely needs the blue pill which I said we had for sale at discounted prices."

Me: "Pete and I laid fully clothed next to each other. I blew in his ear, then his hair and slowly moved my right hand down his back to his bottom. Before I knew it, he was on top of me thrusting away. Don't think he finished. Don't think he got much of an erection but there was definitely a smile on his face. I was so happy he did all the work. I just laid there, like I did when I was married."

The most important information that came from our first day in business was that we all were satisfied with our performances, the two hundred dollars we collected as initiation fees, for the blue pills we sold for twenty dollars as the men left and for making four old men very happy.

Chapter Fifteen

We relaxed on the chaises around the pool after dinner. I was drinking a celebratory Diet Coke and Malibu rum while the other gals sipped chardonnay. Pajamas on, makeup off, it was our time to decompress. Looking out over the slatted fence toward the strip, I felt very content, or maybe the rum was the mellowing factor.

Peta sipped her wine and talked proudly of her sexual experiences, probably exaggerating as elderly people tend to do. It's not that we purposely enjoy not telling the truth; it's more that as years go by, truths meld in to fantasies, indistinguishable from our truths.

"Did you know that I was a virgin when I got married?" Peta offered, "Of course, I was only sixteen, but still, that first night was magical."

"Really?" Sophie inquired.

Peta continued to tell her story. "OK, maybe I was a little scared and I do remember it hurting a bit. Actually, I could hardly walk to the bathroom after it was over. Enzo had moved to London from Sicily via Antwerp, and got a job at the London Jewelry Exchange. He was twenty-one and had finished gemology school in The Netherlands."

"I was totally taken with him," she continued. "His Italian accent was thick and oh so sexy. Sometimes, I could hardly understand what he was saying but whatever it was, it made me melt. He was tall, around six feet, dark hair and eyes, thin with chiseled facial features like a lot of Italians have. Oh, he swept me off my feet. We got married in a tiny church with only two guests after dating for a month. Yup, married at sixteen."

After we all agreed that she was so young and the wedding was very fast, Peta took another sip of wine and continued her story. "Did I tell you how we met?" All three roomies shook their heads no. "Almost every night a group of us would sneak out and meet at the Mecca Dance Hall or Tottenham Royal. There was Mary, Evelyn, Beryl and me. We dressed in our best MOD clothes, styled our hair into flips or Bee Hives, plastered on makeup and handed the doorman our fake ID's. Bobby Darren was our favorite singer. Oh how he made us swoon. We danced to the new music from an upcoming British group called The Beatles. I would work up a sweat doing the Twist, Watusi and Frug. What a time! Actually, that's when I realized I could dance."

"And then one night a song by Elvis came on, It's Now or Never, and this handsome young man asked me to dance. It was like a fairy-tale. We fell in love by the time we twisted to Itsy Bitsy Teenie Weenie and practically were engaged by the end of Brenda Lee singing I'm Sorry. We met at the dance halls night after night, and like I said, were married within a month. Poor Enzo came down with a mysterious flu in nineteen-seventy-two and never recovered. We had twelve years together."

Sophie chimed in. "It sounds like it was a great marriage. Can I get anyone a refill?" Since no one answered, Peta continued talking.

"Maybe a good marriage. Definitely not great." Peta answered. "Enzo was a flirt and I suspected he had a fair amount of back door women. Never proved it but between unexplained business meetings and his growing lack of interest in sex with me, I surmised he was getting a bit on the side. We grew apart. I became angry. He became defensive. I was twenty-eight when he died."

"So sorry," Bernie said as she sipped what was left of her Chardonnay and snacked on the bar mix of nuts and pretzels we had bought at Costco.

"Thanks, Bern," Peta continued, "It was around then that I decided to come to the States. I worked at a hat shop to save money and was very careful with the little life insurance Enzo had left me. Within a year, I had enough cash to make the journey to California. It was so exciting but you're not going to believe what happened within an hour of arriving at Los Angeles International."

"What happened, Peta?" Sophie asked with a bit too much enthusiasm probably caused by the effects of the alcohol.

"I was robbed." Peta said slowly in one of her usual dramatic ways.

"No." All the girls simultaneously gasped at Peta's revelation.

"Yup! While on the curb waiting for a cab, this guy grabbed my neck purse, you know the one you wear to secure your money, and ran off with it. Almost strangled me. He got most of my savings but thankfully, my passport was secure in my fanny pack. Molly, you're awfully quiet"

"I'm just taking it all in, Peta." Molly said as she crunched another handful of bar mix. "This is all new information. I've heard a little about your past but nothing like what you're sharing. Keep going."

"It feels good to share." Peta continued her story.

"I flagged down a policeman and gave a report and

description of the robber. Didn't even have a phone number or address where they could contact me if they caught the bum. Way before cell phones. Finally, I got a cab and as we were leaving the airport area, I saw a sign saying Dancers Wanted. The poor driver. I screamed for him to stop, grabbed my one suitcase and entered the club. After a short interview and dance audition with Bert, the manager, I was hired as a hostess/dancer."

"Good for you." Molly added. Peta gave her a side glance and continued.

"I loved the other girls I met there and actually roomed with a gal named Donna. She was sweet and had a specialty of doing a vertical split on the pole. All the girls had their own stories. Most were running away from something or someone. We supported each other like family."

Peta got up to get another Chardonnay, her third, and asked if anyone else needed a refill. Bernie replied that she did and handed over her glass. I got up to pee and Sophie went to the refrigerator for an ice cream sandwich. When we all had stretched and reclaimed our seats, Peta continued.

"By my second week at the club, I started to date Bert. He understood that my lap and pole dancing were purely business and didn't seem jealous of the hoots and cat calls. Bert didn't have the looks that Enzo had but he did rescue me and I felt somewhat indebted. Soon, I moved out of Donna's flat and in with Bert. And a few months later, we were married. This time it was here, in Las Vegas at The Chapel of Bliss. Sadly, as my popularity got greater, he did become jealous. Five years into our marriage, it was a Saturday, he collapsed. The autopsy didn't give any answers and I never did find out what caused his death. I personally think he was skimming from the cash register and the mob owner had him taken out with some undetectable poison."

"Mob owner?" I asked and then continued. "What kind of people were you working for?" Peta's story was quite unbelievable to me.

"I know," Peta continued, "it sounds like a movie but those clubs can be cesspools of lowlife gangsters. And that's where Harry comes in. He was one of the club's owners. I really don't know for sure if Harry was mob but he sure dressed and sounded like it. You know, with that thick New York accent and his love for pizza. He looked like Clint Eastwood with a little Marlon Brando and James Gandolfini thrown in."

"I like pizza," Sophie interrupted.

"I know you do, Sophie," Peta answered. "But Harry was obsessed with anything Italian, especially Sicilian food. Since I needed employment, I stayed at the club after Bert's death and pleaded with Harry for more hours hosting and less dancing. Within a few months, he was hitting on me. I rejected him and actually started dating a man named Bruce who was a razor salesman from Oklahoma City but came to L.A. often on business. But by nineteen-eighty, Harry had worn me down saying that it was him or my job was gone. So, in a civil ceremony at City Hall, we got married. I needed that job."

Sophie, Bern and I all said that we knew she was going to marry Harry. A sexy, handsome, strong, cigar smoking New Yorker was hard to resist.

"Right from the beginning," Peta continued, "Harry was brutal. He both verbally and physically abused me. Funny thing about being married to a man who calls you everything from a whore to a cunt, and slaps you around while making you strip topless for customers, is that the hold that he had on me grew stronger with every ruthless attack. I was afraid to stay but more afraid to leave. It took me fourteen more years before I was free. Harry died on my fiftieth birthday."

I asked how he died. Peta didn't answer but after taking another swig of wine, continued her story.

"Harry's partner, Stan, made me manager of the place. I worked hard and stayed single for two years until Sly came on the scene. He was a liquor distributor for Bacardi. What can I say, I missed being with a man. He wooed me with flowers, candy and rum. We married at the club with Stan and my friend Donna giving us away. I think because Sly traveled so much, our marriage seemed to work. His territory was the Southwest and only landed in Los Angeles once every two weeks. Our two or three days together were mostly steamy sex with breaks only to eat and shower. He gave me an allowance to supplement my salary. I constantly begged him to change jobs so we could be together all the time and year after year, he promised. His excuse was that he never could find a position that would pay him what he was making. I even suggested I leave the club for a better paying job. He adamantly was against that. So, I stayed and we continued our part time marriage. Have to say that when we were together, it was wonderful. This went on for years, actually, twelve. Then one day a woman came in to the club asking if Sly had been there yet with his delivery. I said no and asked who she was. That was the end of Sly. He was married to that gal, lived in New Mexico through our entire marriage, had three kids and two dogs. Before I could hire an attorney, Sly was found dead on Route 66 just outside of Flagstaff.

That's when I quit the club, moved to Van Nuys, started waitressing for the few years until I was sixty-five and began collecting Social Security and met you all at line dancing. I believe that was 2015."

All of us sat spellbound. We knew Peta had an interesting past but nothing like what we just heard. One by one we got up and gave our roomy a hug. She had survived an adulterer, an abuser, a threatening mob figure and a polygamist. No wonder she clung to our friendship like glue on paper. She needed us for stability and we needed her for inspiration.

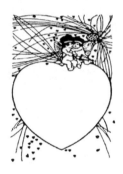

Chapter Sixteen

W e had been open only a month and business was booming. Each day brought at least nine or ten men knocking at our door, many repeat customers, which netted us over four thousand dollars in four weeks. If our numbers kept up at this pace, we would be in entrepreneur success heaven and surely able to afford a whopping great summer vacation.

"Yes, baby! That's perfect. Keep it up! I'm coming home!" A male voice came thundering from Bernie's bedroom. After about five minutes, both the smiling client and Bernie came down the hallway, with the screamer happily booking another appointment.

"I had a strange request." Bernie admitted as she gulped a protein drink in the kitchen. "He asked me to bite him on his ass."

"So?" I asked. "Did you?"

"I did, over his jockeys, of course," Bernie continued. Wasn't sure if he liked it or not but I kept nibbling away. So strange."

We all agreed it was successful based on the shrieks that came from her room a few minutes earlier.

It was obvious that we were heavily intrenched in the pleasure business. I was quite surprised the girls showed no signs of guilt, embarrassment or apprehension. Guess we all were happy with the end results which delivered us the finances to start living a worry-free life. It's interesting how financial security gives one strength and power. None of us had a strong purpose before moving in together. Now, we had jobs and working from home. I was loving being the club's CEO, CFO and COO and quite proud that I had figured out how to bypass the law by not operating as a business. We had no license or permits. We reported to no one. Gifts or donations as we called payment, seemed to be genius on my part. I had no intention of writing off any part of the house as a tax deduction and since the blue pills were purchased in Mexico, there was no tracing them. All seemed to be in order.

It had been a while since I had seen my family. I did make that quick trip back to California during Chanukah and now, they were all coming to visit me for the weekend. This presented quite a dilemma. Stanley knew they couldn't stay with us and had made hotel reservations at The Venetian. But how would I continue business when my son, daughter-in-law and grandson could pop in at any time? I had to figure out the sensitive ballet between visitors and clients.

"Should we shut down for the weekend, ladies?" I was asking my roommates' opinion. "I know they will want to come over and honestly, I want them to see our place."

We all agreed that the weekend days would be client free but while I was out dining and shopping with the family at night, the girls could accept appointments with Peta handling donations and confidentiality papers.

I met Stanley and family at The Cheesecake Factory in Caesars on Friday afternoon around five. Over a very caloric dinner, we gabbed about life in Vegas and our baking business which Stanley believed we were still doing. I explained that business was quite stable and we were taking in enough money to get by. He asked if I was finding myself, using air quotes to emphasize the dig he was making, and I simply said yes and that it was a very exciting and adventurous time in my life. He didn't understand how baking could be exciting.

"Sweetheart," I said, "you never know who will show up at your door and how it will feel to give them something imminently satisfying." He still looked puzzled and I loved my double entendre. We then walked The Forum Shops where I bought grandson Ben a Roman helmet and sword and Stanley kept repeating, "My mother the baker. Pops would not have understood." I thought to myself, Stanley was so right.

"Look, Nana, the ceiling is changing. It's getting dark. Why?" Ben asked.

I explained that it slowly changes from day to night and back again about every hour. All done with computers.

"But how? I know computers but I still don't understand." he asked again and again in a way a child does to demand an answer. He was fascinated by the ceiling, wanted to know the technical mechanics of how it was done and all I wanted was to get home.

"Nana needs to get some rest. I'm sure Mom and Dad can explain it to you. They're very smart. Tomorrow you'll come for lunch at my house and then we'll go back to your hotel for a swim in the big pool. Mine is so small. Okay, darling?"

I had to get out of there. Lying to my son was not something I was comfortable doing. I was a Girl Scout sixty-five years ago and it stuck. After making a quick stop at the grocery store to pick up cheese and bread for the grilled cheese sandwiches I would make the next day, I arrived home to find the girls had entertained two regulars and were rewarding themselves with a late-night dessert.

"How did it go, ladies," I asked with motherly concern.

Peta complained that a guy ejaculated all over her chest. "Wasn't expecting that and to be honest, it wasn't fun. Should have insisted he buy one of our condoms. I immediately showered."

Bernie chimed in that when you let a man motor boat your boobs and lick your tits it's bound to happen. "Maybe keep it to just fondles and kisses," she offered.

I announced that my family would be coming for lunch and asked everyone to put out the family pictures in their bedrooms that we daily put away so clients didn't see anything of our personal life and to hide absolutely everything that looked, smelled or suggested sex.

Sophie shoved another large spoonful of chocolate mousse into her mouth, looked at us intently and spoke. "I have a confession to make. Joe has been here at least ten times to cuddle and kiss and guess what, I think I'm falling in love with him."

With that bombshell, Bern, Peta and I looked at each other, stuffed our faces with a heaping spoonful of mousse and in unison said "Oy Vey."

And that, my friends, is the problem with intimacy. Women jump from a kiss, to love, to visions of a wedding.

Chapter Seventeen

Twelve sharp and the doorbell rang. I had left Stanley's name at the communities' guard gate and they gave him directions to the house. Ben ran in, looked at the pool through the kitchen sliding doors and immediately wanted to swim. "Not now, sweetheart." I instructed. "The pool is not heated during the winter. Too expensive. We're going to have lunch and then go to your beautiful hotel to swim. I'm sure they keep it nice and warm. Hungry?"

The girls all greeted my kids and gracefully left saying they had prior engagements at one of the clubs. I showed everyone around and got Stanley's approval of the house. "Have to admit it's nice, Ma. Glad you are happy."

I cooked six grilled cheese sandwiches stuffed with onions and tomato and served them with Costco's Tomato Basil soup. Good lunch with no inquisitions.

As we were just about ready to leave for the Strip, the doorbell rang three times. That was the code I had established for our Club. A man I recognized as a regular client of Peta's was folding his walker against the porch entry wall and started to come in as Stanley yelled from the kitchen questioning who it was.

"It's just a neighbor," I called back.

"I'm not actually a neighbor," the man replied, adding, "You know me, Molly. I have a standing every Saturday at two. Is she ready for me? I took a pill and I'm really ready for her."

My heart sank as Stanley came to the door and asked if he could help the gentleman with anything. The client paused, surveyed my son, then promptly replied that he had never tried it with a man but was up for a new adventure. Stanley looked at me with a very disturbed frown as I jumped in and said, "It's Bill, right? You have your days mixed up. Peta teaches chocolate chip cookie making on Monday, not Saturday. Have a nice day dear and we'll see you in a couple of days." With that, I slammed the door and whisked Stanley back to the kitchen. Poor Bill. I'm sure he was totally confused and certain dementia had kicked in.

Meanwhile, Ben had opened a top cabinet and unscrewed a canister. "Nana, can I have some of these blue mints? They look pretty good."

OMG! Ben had gotten into the jar where we stored the Viagra. "No," I screamed just as he was about to eat the found candy. "They are a strong condiment for baking and not to be eaten raw or your stomach may explode. Put it back." I grabbed Ben, my purse and jacket. "Everyone ready to go? Let's move on. Please."

I'm sure Stanley thought my reactions were over the top but I felt I had salvaged the lunch with no obvious indications that they had eaten grilled cheese in a house of sexual pleasure.

The rest of the weekend went unscathed. Saturday night we ate dinner out, saw a show at Circus Circus, took Ben to Treasure Island and watched the dancing fountains at Bellagio. It was good being with family. They made me smile and gave me hugs of love. Ben always grabbed my hand as we walked and told me delicious stories about school and his friends. Some of the tales were hysterical with hijinks only nine-year-old boys could think up. Being with this young man brought joy to my heart. My family knew my past and the comfort of talking about what was and who was there filled a very empty space.

Peta admitted she had forgotten to cancel Bill and apologized profusely. I accepted the apology and we had a laugh at the near catastrophe it caused. I suggested we give Bill a free visit to amend the mistake.

Now it was time to deal with Sophie and her professed love. I remember vividly Belle at the Chicken Ranch saying it was a strict rule that her girls did not get romantically involved with the clientele. We needed to adhere to the same decree if our little palace of amour was to survive.

It was Sunday night and my family had gone back to Los Angeles. After going through the schedule of clients that had booked for the week ahead, we all sat around the living room drinking tea and noshing on huge red seedless grapes. Funny how we four took the same seats every time; Sophie and Bernie on the flowered sofa, Peta on the brown leather lounger and me on the blue club chair. No matter what the occasion, we were drawn to our same special spot.

"So, Sophie," I started. "Please tell us about this guy you like. What's been going on?"

Sophie shared that she and Joe just felt so comfortable together and that they would lay on the bed, arms around each other and share stories. "Sometimes he would softly kiss me on the cheek, then lips, my eyes and neck. It's been so romantic. I've never had this kind of tender love before."

Peta interrupted. "You were married for years. Sol wasn't romantic?"

"No," Sophie continued. "After our baby died, he became very distant. And after my father died and willed us, rather me, his business, Sol just concentrated on making money. He had worked for my father most of our married life, as an associate producer, and then when we, actually I, inherited the production company, Sol became obsessed with creating his own fortune. We would go for months without making love. I think the longest was around six. One night I walked in on him masturbating in the bedroom closet. I was furious and hurt and confused. Why wasn't I good enough or pretty enough for him to want sexually? We went to counseling briefly but that didn't help. He just got more obsessed with the business year after year and less interested in me. When the company had a few failures and no studio would back our films, that's when he started selling points to investors. Before I knew it, Sol had gone through the millions Dad had left me and we were almost penniless. We were still living high and spending like millionaires when in reality, he was selling everything in sight to make payments.

"I'm so sorry," Peta said, giving Sophie a big hug. "How did it end?"

Sophie took another gulp of tea and continued. "When a lady in Tarzana became friends with another woman at jazzercise class and over lunch compared what they thought were exciting investments, life quickly unraveled. They contacted other people who they knew had invested in some of the films and finally investigative accountants were brought in. Books and computers were confiscated for evidence, depositions taken and boom, Sol was arrested for fraud. Through the entire trial I stood by him. He was convicted and sent to jail never once saying sorry for the emotional pain, let alone financial disaster, he caused me. I loved him when we got married but despised him by the time he died in prison. No, there was no romance."

"When did you divorce him," I asked.

"It took a year but I filed shortly after he was sent away. He humiliated me. What did I get from giving him my life? No love. No child. No security. Joe is gentle and a good man. I want to experience that kind of love before I die."

To hell with rules. We encouraged Sophie to have any kind of relationship with Joe she desired. Rules? We were writing our own.

Chapter Eighteen

There were three clients waiting in the living room. All were new to our Club, had signed the confidentiality agreement and made their monetary donations. Jake would be doing the bump and grind with me. Steve would be getting an over his Bermuda shorts hand job from Bernie and Peta was scheduled to let Peter play with her tits.

I took Jake to my bedroom and asked Alexa to play some light jazz. "So, Jake, there's some Kleenex on the dresser in case you have a happy ending. Want to get undressed or do this with your clothes on? I stay dressed. I also have condoms if you think you'll cum."

Jake didn't answer but sat on the ottoman at the foot of the bed and just starred at me. "Ok, fellow, this is your first time here and I'm presuming you're a bit nervous. Right?" Jake didn't answer so I continued. "Come on to the bed. I won't bite you." I laughed thinking that I just might if things got a bit kinky. He looked so meek but those are the ones you needed to be cautious of. "Come on cutie pie. I don't have all day."

"Why are you doing this?" he finally asked.

"Why are you here?" I responded.

"Well," Jake continued clearing his throat, "I've been wanting to meet you for months. I see you playing Bunco at Clubhouse Three but didn't know if you wanted to meet a man. Then Glenn gave me your card. I don't want to dry hump you. I want to date you."

I sat on the side of the bed totally in shock. My head got light and I had to steady myself with both hands. It was bad enough that Sophie was seeing Joe on the side but me date a Club member? I hadn't had a real date in almost seven years. There was the accountant that I met on Match but that was a onetime coffee. Hardly call that a date.

Jake waited for my answer. His right leg was shaking like he was nervously pumping up a pool floaty. Poor Jake. He wasn't the handsomest man in this community of old souls. Maybe five feet seven, shoulders that slouched forward, almost totally bald except for that fringe that circled his head. But he did have blue eyes that showed he was sweet and a smile that curled his lips at each end.

"Yes," I answered to my surprise. "I'd love to have lunch or dinner or coffee with you. But my business partners can't know. So, does this mean you want your donation refunded?"

My prospective suiter just grinned and told me to keep it so I'd be indebted to him. "I'll call you," he said as he opened the bedroom door and sauntered down the hall with a little limp and a proud as a peacock attitude.

I had just added another layer of complication to an already complex business. Maybe Jake was like the Richard Gere character in Pretty Woman who wanted to rescue the tough but needy hooker? No matter what his motive, it would be our secret. The girls could not know. Dating Jake would be on the down low. I'm pretty sure I used that terminology correctly. Right?

Chapter Nineteen

This was our fourth date. Jake and I had gone out for coffee, had dinner atop the Paris Hotel's Eiffel Tower and gone to see a Cirque du Soleil performance. Tonight, he was cooking dinner at his home which was on the opposite side of our development

"I just need some alone shopping therapy." That was my go-to lie. The ladies still had no idea I was seeing someone. I knew this little elfin man was some sort of a financial/business startup man in his pre-retirement life and a widower. But other than that, I had gathered little information. He didn't share much and I was content not to ask. Three dates down.

I've heard that sex was expected now-a-days on the third date. We had just held hands. Tonight, I suspected would be different. I wore a light blue cotton very tailored pant suit and accessorized with a long strand of pearls with matching earrings. Jake had on his usual tan chinos and a light green Ralph Lauren polo shirt. Was this the night we would make love? I hadn't had sex in over nine years. And believe it, or not, I was a virgin when I married Sam. Nervous wreck didn't begin to quantify my state of mind.

Senior sex is different. Before Sam got sick, we had a routine – Saturday night out to dinner, usually Chinese, come home, watch two hours of television, take Viagra at ten thirty and have sex at eleven. Our positions complimented whatever aches we had at the moment. But most often, it was missionary style with him climaxing way before I was even a little hot. Sometimes he would help my coital frustration and take me to an unromantic finish but most often, he would roll off and kiss me goodnight.

We're not as flexible in our sixties or seventies and definitely not eighties as we were in our early years. And our stamina is suspect. I think the word that epitomizes senior sex is tender rather than passionate. Oh, the mental road map of passion is there but the reality of performing like a horny rabbit has long left the farm house.

"I think it's time we talked." Jake said as he plated the salad and salmon.

"Sure," I responded. "About what? I'd love to hear more about your life."

"You know, your business." Jake poured some chardonnay as he continued.

I tried to change the subject by asking about the unusual painting over the fireplace. Jake didn't sway. "Molly, I'd like to know why you have this club, as you call it. Not only am I jealous of the other men having sex with you but I'm petrified you're going to get arrested or worse, get some horrible sexual disease. And then what?"

"My, my," I answered. "You don't mince words, do you? First of all, it's really none of your business what I do in my private time. But if you must know, I view this little club as a public service. Almost a charity for lonely men. None of us girls have real sex with anyone, only pretend sex. It's like high school petting. And getting caught? Not afraid. I'm not charging. And we're adults doing fun adult things. My son is an attorney. He doesn't know about my life in Vegas but if anything were to happen, he'd come to my rescue."

Jake took another sip of wine and let me continue without saying a word. "Look, Jake, it's complicated. This club is like my baby. I conceived the idea, I nurtured it through its infancy and now that it's getting to be successful, I'm proudly reaping the rewards which are purely financial. And the benefits go far beyond security for the girls and me. It's a feather in my gray hair and I need and want the satisfaction of doing something with my life. I was always the second fiddle in my household. No more. I want to be the first chair in this orchestra of life while I can still appreciate the music."

"That's quite the convoluted explanation," Jake said.

"We're not harming anyone or anything, Jake." I continued my explanation. "It's the only thing all of us are good at. Pleasing men. Think of us as community social workers." I was passionate. "It's your turn, Jake. How did you wind up in Vegas?"

Jake tapped on the table a few times in a nervous, not musical way, cleared his throat and spoke. "She always wanted to live where it's warm. She loved the slot machines. So, we packed up and moved from

Cleveland. This was after she was diagnosed with Stage 3 breast cancer. At first all was great. Chemo had worked and she took her meds religiously. We joined clubs, made some friends and were enjoying retirement."

"Sounds wonderful, Jake. She beat it." I offered.

"Not so fast, Molly." Jake responded. "True, all was great for about a year. And then it changed. The cancer had spread to her stomach and she was gone. The kids wanted me to come home to Cleveland but I convinced them that this was where I was comfortable. I see them twice a year. My grandkids are twelve and fifteen. My son didn't follow my path in finance and is a chemical engineer specializing in bio-tech. My daughter is also married, no kids and is a teacher."

"Do you miss her, your wife?" I asked.

Jake took my hand and held it in his. "Everyday. Just like I assume you miss Sam."

I finished my glass of wine just as Jake got up from his seat. I wasn't sure if he was going to escort me out the front door or ask me to do the dishes in the kitchen. I was wrong on both accounts. He helped me out of my chair, gently kissed me on the cheek and walked me to his bedroom. Oh, that room needed a woman's touch but at least the bed was made and the sheets looked clean.

Jake didn't waste any time taking off his shirt and then slowly unbuttoning my blue top. When he saw I wasn't objecting, a quick stroll to the bed was next. Off came his trousers, my bra and my slacks. Amazingly, I wasn't embarrassed or even bashful. Under the cover, we both removed the remaining vestiges of our clothing and began the dance of love making. It was the first time for both of us since our beloved spouses had died. It was a bit strange, a bit uncomfortable at first, but wonderful to know that we both still had a working libido.

I had so many more questions for Jake, but it was certainly not the time or place. He made it clear that it was our spouses who had died and not us. We deserved to be loved and oh, what a lover Jake turned out to be. He was generous, tender, confident and knew his way around a climax – or two!

Chapter Twenty

Why do so many people think senior sex is strange? Yuck, as a twelve-year-old would say. Research shows that desire is key to fulfillment with perhaps a little help from pharmaceuticals. After several months of running our Club, we all noticed that the most important element in what men have requested of us is touch.

A simple hug, a soothing hand to hold, a caress that says you are important. Our clients crave intimacy of a humble nature.

Of course, there are those few who want more. We've only had one incident where a client got a bit too bizarre. Actually, very bizarre. That was with dear

Bernie. I'll let her tell you the story in her own words. Take it away, Bern.

"As you all know, my specialty has been fondling and blow jobs. About three weeks ago I accepted an appointment with a man I'll call Frank. He showed up at four thirty, paid his donation, signed the confidentiality agreement and followed me down the hall to my bedroom.

"So Frank, let's cuddle on the bed. Kissing and touching is fine but watch your tongue and hands. If it gets too frisky, I'll pull away and your session will be over. Got it?" Frank nodded and asked if I would sit on his lap for a bit. Said he just wanted to hold me. That sounded very innocent and I obliged by taking my shoes off, unbuttoning the two top buttons of my pink floral blouse and sitting across his lap with my feet on the ground. Before I knew it, this insane man pulled my legs up and held me like a baby. "You're so sweet, so innocent. Daddy loves you." He said the love part several times. When I tried to change my position, he quickly held my wrists. I started to shout but he threatened that if I did, he would harm me.

"Just relax, my baby, I'm not going to hurt you." With that, he carried me to the bed, took off his shirt and tried to pull my slacks down. Luckily, my feet were nimble. I kicked him with all my might in the balls, jumped off the bed and ran out of the bedroom toward the living room screaming at the top of my lungs.

"We have a crazy in my bedroom. Help me." I was gasping for breath. "This is too hard. Molly, you finish the story," Bernie took a deep breath as I gave her a hug.

I picked up from that point and recounted what happened next. "As soon as I heard Bernie scream, I seized the kitchen scissors, grabbed a frying pan and the can of mace on the counter next to the toaster and sprinted down the hall."

When I burst into her room, this Frank guy was sitting on the bed crying like a two-year old, wiping his tears with what looked like his sock. He was absolutely startled to see me with mace in one hand and a cast-iron pan in the other and immediately started to apologize."

"I'm so sorry," he said. "I wouldn't have hurt her. Her face. Those eyes. It's how my wife looked. But she's dead." I put down the pan and quickly realized I was dealing with a very disturbed man. Frank apologized a million times and said it was the fifth anniversary of her death. I admonished him for acting out and scaring a dear woman and warned him that he must never come anywhere near this house again. He kept nodding that he understood.

"Frank, your membership has been revoked. If I see you anywhere even close to this vicinity again, I'll get a restraining order to keep you away." That, of course, was a bunch of bull since the last thing I wanted was to involve the police.

"Now put on your shirt, leave through the sliding glass door, turn left, go out the side gate and wipe today from your brain. Bernie will be fine. You, on the other hand, desperately need help."

I poured Bern a glass of the pinot grigio she liked. "Let's sit by the pool and try to relax until Sophie and Peta are back from the market. We need to have a serious talk."

With the groceries put away, I caught Sophie and Peta up on the disturbing events of the day.

"How are you doing, Bernie?" Peta asked. All four of us sat on the patio, trying to understand the bizarre event.

Bernie thought for a moment and answered. "I'll be alright. I've been through worse."

"What do you mean?" I inquired. "That must have been frightening."

Bernie got up and turned her lounge chair to face the sun. "I've been hit on a lot. You know, in my younger years, when I was modeling. But never by a crazed maniac who thought I was his dead wife. I wanted to scream that I know what it's like to lose a spouse. Hell, I lost two kids in the accident plus my husband. But I was in such shock that the words just didn't come out."

We all nodded that we understood. Bernie continued. "I was on my way home from a doctor's appointment. Had a sinus infection. Just as I pulled into the driveway, I saw the police cars. A female cop came up to me as I opened my car door and told me there had been an accident. Funny, I don't remember what she said next. Guess I just collapsed. So many years and I still wait for Mack to come through the door."

I joined Bernie at the foot of the lounge chair. "Do you think we should call it quits?" I looked at the others for a decision, or at least confirmation that after what happened that day, our business was just too risky.

Bernie was the first to comment. "No. I may take a few days off but this one nut job is not going to scare me to the point of quitting something that is fun and may I add, profitable. Not to worry ladies, I'll be just fine."

Sophie had been relatively quiet. "I'm not too sure going ahead is a good idea," she said. "There probably are other crazies out there. How can we be certain this or something worse won't happen again? What if he had a weapon?"

She had a point. There was no guarantee. We were taking chances every time we allowed a fellow community resident into our bedroom. "Karate." I said. "That's the answer. Let's all take some self defense classes so we feel empowered and safe. Sound good? I'll find us a class or a private teacher."

"Brilliant." Peta chimed in. "That way if a fellow gets out of hand, we can deck him or even kill him."

I exclaimed that killing was definitely out of the question which made me think again about all of Peta's dead husbands. "I'll get on it right away. There has to be someone who can teach us how to be Ninjas."

154

Chapter Twenty-One

G oogle led me to self defense classes in Las Vegas which led me to courses in Jiu Jitsu, Kick Boxing, Mixed Martial Arts and Krav Maga. We chose a free course offered by a local women's center which would teach us basic defense moves to get out of most aggressive situations and started, coincidentally, the next day.

I put an outgoing message on my work cell that we were closed for a long weekend and to call back next week. Dressed in sweat pants and exercise clothes of varying colors and styles, Sophie, Bernie and I were ready to fight and win. Of course, Peta wore purple spandex.

It was a two-day program that taught us moves to thwart an aggressive attacker from the back or front and how to take even the largest of men down. It was empowering, exhausting and fun – except for the aches we all felt the day after.

Bernie did feel much safer after the classes as did the rest of our group. Just learning where to kick (the balls), where to punch (the Adams Apple), where to stomp (the instep of a foot) defused our fears and gave us the strength to continue with business. Being able to say and believe that we were in control was huge. Thank you, Alliance for Women's Safety. The group should have been called Alliance for Kicking Ass.

I was seeing Jake at least three times a week. If it wasn't at night, we would meet for brunch or just for a drive along the strip. Little by little, he opened up more about his past. He had been the lead finance person for a large drug company and had actually invented several container products that he held patents on.

"Oh, how I love the Las Vegas summer heat. Can't wait for July." he would say sarcastically with a little chuckle. I'd laugh along with him and say that I was happy to contribute by adding some additional heat to his fire. And hot I was! It had been so long since I had experienced adult love. Male interactions with the club were different. I would be on robot mode when I had clients or had to pinch in. If Sophie had a cold, I'd do the cuddles. But if Bernie or Peta were under the weather, I couldn't bring myself to do hand jobs or tits, especially since I met Jake. I would just cancel the appointments and reschedule.

Jake was making everything different. I did explain to him that business was just a means to an end. It's a very confident man that could accept that. And I adored that confidence. On our long walks or dinners or rides out to Hoover Dam I'd quiz him until he would finally give me answers. On his own, away from his day job, he had been constantly creating and inventing which I secretly envied. Maybe someday we would create something together; something monumental that would change the world. I caught myself day dreaming that we fashioned an amazing product so I could shut down the Club and become CEO of a different type of business. Dreams are fun but can also be dangerous. I'd stop myself thinking that what was real now was what I had to put my energy in to.

Meanwhile, Sophie was dating Joe openly. They would go out to dinner and a movie, or dancing or to a show at one of the hotels. Sophie was smitten and we all were happy for her.

"I only hope you all find companionship like I have," Sophie would say. Little did she or my other two roomies know that my secret companionship included mind blowing sex with a man who had an IQ of 158.

Chapter Twenty-Two

Spring brought more customers. Business was booming and we were raking in dough like we never imagined. Joe and I were still seeing each other and my roommates were none the wiser. I loved having a big secret. It made me feel mysterious, like a heroine in a Bogart film.

The fact that we had been able to keep the Club going for all of these months was amazing. No one ratted us out. Customers seemed to be happy and there were no further scary client incidents to worry us. I finally had success. It was a long time coming, like 73 years, but it was here and my best friends and I were reaping the rewards. For the first time in my life, I was proud of me.

Our supply of Mexican Viagra was running a bit low and a trip back to Tijuana was planned for early Fall. With the heat rising in Las Vegas and customers taking off to far away places visiting family and vacation spots, we looked forward to some down time and a summer vacation of our own.

Sophie and Joe planned a road trip to San Diego in late June and a long drive up the California coast. They couldn't wait to spend time at the zoo and Joe wanted to explore the USS Midway Museum. Sophie wanted to shop in Carmel. Peta planned to go back to Britain to see friends and promised Bernie she could come along. I told the gals that I was just going to my son's home for an extended visit when in actuality Jake and I had reservations for an Alaskan cruise and tour of Canada.

Everything seemed to be as it should until a knock on our door in early May brought things to a screeching halt.

"Miss Shapiro?" Peta stood at the door and starred at the officer. "No," Peta said. "I'll get her. What's this about?"

The uniformed officer said that he needed to speak to Miss Shapiro.

"Molly," Peta screamed while surveying the officer. "A policeman is here and wants to speak to you." Peta took a beat and said to the husky man sweating through his shirt, "And it's Mrs. Shapiro. She's widowed. As am I and our other roommates. What's this about, anyway?"

The officer didn't answer.

Molly came around the corner from her bedroom and halted with a sense of possible danger when she saw the uniformed man. "Sir, what can I do for you?"

The officer proceeded to explain that their neighbor, Mrs. Sarkowsky, called in a report that something fishy was going on in our house. She apparently told one of our community security guards that a large number of men had been coming and going from our house for months, sometimes three or four at a time. The guard called the Las Vegas PD.

Peta started to object but I immediately said "I'll deal with this. Why don't you go start the barbecue while Officer, ugh." I didn't know the man's name.

"Officer Lange. I should have introduced myself properly," he answered with a type of authority that was neither scary or friendly.

"Well, Officer Lange," I answered, "Let's sit down in the living room where it's cool and I'll be happy to answer any questions you have."

The officer walked in and took a seat in the blue club chair. I felt like saying that's my seat but erased that idea and sat on the couch.

"Mrs. Shapiro, are you doing anything illegal here? Your neighbor, Mrs. Sarkowsky, seems to think you are." The Officer didn't mince words. "She says there's a lot of activity with men going on. Can you explain?"

I was amazingly calm and answered, "Illegal? Why no, sir. If Mrs. Sarkowsky questioned why we have men visiting us, or why she sees walkers lined up on the front porch, she should have just come over and inquired. What she saw were members of our club. We have this group where we play games and I bake cookies and we talk about our lives. It's totally innocent. What a nosy woman. I'll think twice about inviting her over for canasta or dominoes."

"Do you keep a log of the men who come by, Mrs. Shapiro?"

I answered a strong no.

The officer continued. "Your neighbor seems to think you're running some kind of gambling establishment or a sex den. Are you, Mrs. Shapiro?"

I chuckled and answered that whatever Mrs. Sarkowsky thinks is going on here is absurd and that she had best mind her own business or my son the lawyer would be slapping a suit against her for slander.

Of course, I had no idea what constituted a slanderous case but it sounded like I did.

Officer Lange got up and walked around the room. On the counter between the kitchen and living room was a dish with about twenty Viagra pills in it. He stopped, checked out the dish and asked, "Are these blue pills Viagra?"

I quickly answered, "Why on earth would four old ladies have that sitting out in the open? They are fake Viagra pills that I got at that fun store on Flamingo. It's candy. A mint. Want one?" I prayed he'd say no and put one in my mouth for evidence.

The policeman shook his head no and said he'd tell my neighbor that we seemed like lovely women and thanked me for my time. He continued, "But Mrs. Shapiro, we'll be keeping an eye on the house and you, so make sure there really isn't anything fishy going on. Have a good day."

As soon as he closed the door, I spit out the Viagra in the kitchen sink and gulped down a large glass of apple juice to get rid of the bitter pill taste while wondering if I'd get turned on. Sadly, I didn't.

Chapter Twenty-Three

We ignored our neighbor's suppositions and carried on with our Senior Sex Club for the next few weeks. Although, I have to admit it was a bit scary. We limited visitors to three at a time and asked the men using walkers to park them in inside our entry. No more pool parties. We told a few trusted clients what occurred and all swore they knew nothing about the neighbor who ratted on us.

By the end of May the temperature was hovering around ninety-five and many of our Club members were heading to cooler climates for the summer. By Memorial Day, we informed the brave souls who were staying behind, sweltering in triple digit heat, that we would be closing down until Labor Day.

I was so looking forward to getting away. The four of us did research on how to summerize the house. For those of you not living in hellish hot weather, that means putting plastic over the toilet bowl seats so the water doesn't evaporate, unplugging clocks, small appliances and televisions, setting the air conditioner to eighty-four, placing large containers of water around the house to create humidity and putting our pool guy on notice to only come once a week.

It was the day everyone was leaving. One by one my roomies departed. Hugs, kisses and promises of taking lots of photos and sending emails extended our goodbyes by at least a half hour. Four amigos. Four old ladies off on another adventure because we allowed ourselves to be hugged.

Jake arrived at the house around two in the afternoon, a few hours after they all left. We would take a flight to Seattle at ten-thirty the next morning and immediately board our Princess cruise. I couldn't wait.

We never made it to the ship. We never left Las Vegas.

Around ten in the evening, two uniformed Las Vegas police officers arrived at my door. They didn't explain much and said they were taking me in for questioning. Before when Officer Lange came to the house, he had no evidence that my roommates or I had done anything illegal, no charges had been filed. This time seemed different and more aggressive.

"What is this all about?" Jake demanded from the Officers. He was confused and wanted answers. He tried to console me but wasn't allowed to give me even a little hug. "Don't worry sweetheart. I'm sure this is a mistake. You'll be home in a few hours."

"Call my son." I shouted to Jake as I was loaded into the back of the police car. "His number is on the refrigerator. He'll take care of everything. If I'm allowed a phone call, I'll call him, too."

"I love you." Jake blurted out.

Did I hear that right or was I hallucinating? Did this elfin man just say he loves me as I'm being hauled off in a black and white? It could not have been worse timing.

Salutations of love aside, I had a gut feeling this time my encounter with the police would be different. Was it Mrs. Sarkowsky complaining again. If not her, who?

A bit scared and very embarrassed, I complied with whatever the officers asked while at least ten of my neighbors looked on, some with horror and others with glee, as we started to drive away. The last words I remember hearing was Mrs. Sarkowsky shouting, "I told you so. I told you she was a Madame. Good riddance to stinking fish."

I felt like screaming back that I considered myself a Mistress and certainly not a Madame. But I controlled my urge and sat quietly in the back of the patrol car. Anyway, by the time I thought of my response we were a block away.

Chapter Twenty-Four

"And at the station, I called you. You said Jake had already called and that you were on your way. And now you're here." I was talking to Stanley, my son the lawyer.

The guard stood in the corner fidgeting with his keys. Stanley asked me what the hell I was thinking and asked the guard if we could have some privacy. Absolutely not was the answer. What was he afraid of – a seventy something old lady sawing through bars with the nail file her son had secretly slipped her in a bran muffin?

Pulling his chair as close to the metal table as possible, my son the lawyer leaned in trying to create some modicum of privacy. "So. Ma, you're only here for questioning. You weren't read your Miranda rights so you definitely haven't been arrested. You should be out in a few hours as soon as I clear this whole thing up." When I didn't react, Stanley got up, stretched his arms over his head and again sat down. He didn't look like a successful attorney. In his jeans and very wrinkled plaid shirt he looked tired and more like a Seven Eleven cashier. But what could I expect? The poor guy drove most of the night from Los Angeles to rescue his mother out of jail.

"Ma, you need to start explaining. And include who this Jake fella is. If I'm going to clear this thing up, I need to know what this . . . whatever this . . ."

Stanley was grasping for words. Not his usual eloquent, assured self. After all, the last thing he could have imagined when he went to bed last night was getting a call that his mother was in the slammer on suspected obscenity charges.

175

"Jake? He is my boyfriend. And darling, it's a rather long story."

"Boyfriend? We'll get to that later. Ma, explain." Stanley barked. "I have lots of visiting time with you and nothing else to talk about. What got you brought in for questioning."

I talked. Stanley listened.

"Things were going so well." I cleared my throat and wiped my forehead with my shirt sleeve. I was nervous. "And then, it wasn't. The baking business failed and we had to come up with another idea. We really weren't doing anything so bad. A little hug here or a touch there. Nothing illegal."

Stanley interrupted. "Well Ma, something seemed illegal or you wouldn't be sitting on a metal chair in an interrogation room. What is this business? Were you running a brothel out of your house? That's what the officer said you were doing. You are so lucky I'm licensed in Nevada."

"No!" I protested. "Not exactly. It isn't a brothel. It's a club where men pay dues and get, let's just say their loneliness taken care of. We didn't take any money from them for sex."

Stanley interrupted and challenged what I had just said. "Ma, you said they paid dues."

"I mean, they gave donations. Even for the Viagra." I was agitated that Stanley was being so picky. "We didn't make them pay. They just pocketed the pills as they left and put some money in a jar by the front door."

Stanley just kept shaking his head in disbelief. I continued, "No, we didn't have sex with any of the men, in my definition, and even if we did, that's not illegal.

177

But we didn't. Especially when you consider my liberal meaning of sex.

Intercourse was off the table.

No, we didn't charge for the cuddles or motor boating or dry humping.

Yes, we accepted donations to help keep the club going. Fizzy water and lotions aren't cheap.

No, we didn't have a business license because we weren't a business.

Yes, we did take appointments so each of our members got the attention he deserved."

Another man entered the room and introduced himself as Detective Addison.

"Officer," Stanley asked, "What exactly is my mother being charged with?"

Addison replied, "That's Detective and she's here on possible obscenity charges. Just questioning for now."

"And who brought up these charges, Detective?" My son asked.

The Detective man who looked like a middle-aged chubby boy scout answered that he was not at liberty to say but that they had on very strong assumption that hanky panky was going on in my house. He actually didn't say hanky panky but some other words that were much more legal and demeaning.

Assumption? I was smart enough to know that assumption is not evidence.

Stanley went in to lawyer mode and paced the small interrogation room.

He spoke eloquently in his perfect law school summation voice. Not too strong but with the confidence of someone who knew he would win. I was beaming with Jewish mother pride.

"Officer, assumption? That's not enough to arrest someone." Stanley said with conviction.

"Again, it's Detective and your mother is not arrested, yet. She's here only for questioning since complaints have been filed by several neighbors regarding activities in and around her house."

I breathed a huge sigh of relief hearing I hadn't been actually arrested even though it sure felt like it to me. My son, on the other hand, seemed agitated and was rubbing his forehead.

Stanley finally spoke and was brilliant. He was like Perry Mason (a television lawyer from many years past) and Judge Judy and commanded the small room.

"Morality you see Detective, in the criminal justice system, is defined as a descriptive account of social and personal values about the way people in our society should behave. It's very subjective. The club these women started is serving a monumental life necessity, a basic tenant of existence, the need of a person to be heard, the need to be recognized. And yes, the need to feel the touch of another being. These four brave souls have found a way to not only serve the community in which they live, but to support their very lives. I believe a big misunderstanding is going on here."

Stanley cleared his throat and continued. "You don't have a case against my mother or her roommates. You can't deny a person the right to have social discourse."

And on those eloquent words, my Stanley and I were escorted to the door and I was a free woman. Stanley would come back, if necessary, to represent the other girls and me if charges were ever filed. They weren't. The big question, would I have to shut the club down? The complaints issued against me were civil nuisance and obscenity charges. I guessed they were filed by a customer who wanted more than we were willing to give.

My son the lawyer went back to his family in California departing with the wise words I use to tell him. "Ma, keep your nose clean." And I went back to my empty Las Vegas home. What to do? The entire time of planning and executing the club made me feel important, useful. Now, on Stanley's advice, I had to tell the girls we would be shutting down. Those words – it's too dangerous. He said that it's really only a matter of time until more disgruntled club members turn you in and say they paid for sex. I didn't want to believe him but knew he was right. Our Senior Sex Club would be no longer.

I sat in the living room and commiserated with myself. I had to tell the girls. Do I spoil their vacations? And, poor Jake. We've missed the boat literally. It had sailed just as the police decided to release me. Thank goodness we took out cancelation insurance.

What was I thinking starting a business based on love and connection? What do I know about why humans need to be touched and listened to and encouraged, except for the fact that I am human? I was at my lowest and only had been home for a few hours. My dreams of becoming an uber successful business woman were gone.

Chapter Twenty-Five

J̄ake was stretched out on the couch and I sat quietly in my blue club chair. "What's next?" he asked, sipping on the lemonade I had just brought him.

"I have no idea," I answered pensively. "Of course, I have to tell the girls we're shut down. I'll wait until their vacations are over. Oh, and I have a stash of Viagra to get rid of and enough lotion to lather all four of us until we die."

I looked at Jake for answers but he was quiet. I continued, "Maybe I should move back to California. I'm all out of ideas."

With that, Jake sat upright. "So, you're going to give up, sell the house and go back to five days a week playing board games? Sounds defeatist to me."

Jake was right. I did sound like a woman who had given up. But that's how I felt. The club was my one idea that worked. The fact that it was quite iffy when it came to the law was irrelevant.

"Let's go down to the Strip and get some dinner, sweetheart." Jake said. "My treat. Take your mind off of things."

Never one to reject a hotel dinner, I pulled myself together. Jake decided on Paris. At least if we had to give up Alaska we may as well go to a resort that made us feel like we were on vacation. After checking the car with the valet, we walked through the rather small gambling floor on our way to Mon Ami Gabi for their delicious onion soup.

"Jake," I asked, "what's that on the floor?"

Sure enough, I bent down and picked up a black plastic betting chip. Jake looked at it and informed me that it was worth a hundred dollars.

"Let's bet it," I said. "My luck can only go up from here."

One wager on red led to another on black to another on red seven and so on. I kept putting all my winnings on the next bet with pleas from Jake to stop and cash in my chips. I didn't listen and eventually walked away from the table with over thirty thousand dollars. I was stunned and giddy all at the same time. I had never been a gambler but it sure felt great winning. Yes, winning big time.

Over the best onion soup in the whole world, Jake kept telling me that this was an anomaly and to not become obsessed with casinos. He also said this unexpected windfall was a new opportunity to start another, more main stream, business. Or, he said, just retire and have it as a financial cushion.

Main stream or retire sounded so dull after the club. The basic tenants of my Senior Sex Club were to give others pleasure while raking in some cash. I was good at organizing. I was excellent at putting people together and I was the best at matching someone's needs to what was available.

"That's it," I screamed. "I know what my next venture will be. I have start up cash. I can give jobs to my roommates and between our club clients and the single people we know, we have enough connections to open."

"Open what?" Jake asked cautiously.

"Mistress Molly's Senior Matchmaking Service" I answered. "It's perfect. I can advertise that it's exclusively for lonely old folk. I could make some money, the girls would have jobs and I could help dozens, if not hundreds of single women and men meet eligible partners. I would still call myself Mistress Molly. I like the sound of that. Just think, Jake, how many people I could make happy."

And so, it began. When the girls got home, they were shocked that I had shut down the club but thrilled that I had come up with a new venture. Everyone agreed that matchmaking for the elderly would be a super success in Las Vegas since there were so many senior communities.

I did get a business license this time and rented a small office located just off the strip to conduct in person interviews. Most of my early clients were from my own community, but gradually word spread through the entire city that there was a new matchmaking business just for mature, aging folks.

I hired the same photographer that had done our boudoir pictures to take   photos of all new clients. I advertised in retirement community newsletters. Flyers landed in all the haunts that serve Early Bird dinners. I blanketed the town with info on how to find love after seventy.

Word quickly started to buzz around our Matchmaking service and I began to do local radio shows. By mid-December, we had over a hundred success stories. It was just in time for new lovers to celebrate the holidays together. Love matching. I was born to do this. My picture and some of our success clients were featured in the Las Vegas Review newspaper. I was asked to be on The Morning Blend television show. After that appearance, our numbers skyrocketed.

Apparently, a producer from Shark Tank saw the billboard we had rented advertising our services. It was located right as you enter the city. How could anyone miss the ten feet high and twenty-two feet wide ad of us gals with four handsome elderly guys? We talked and I pitched Molly's Matchmaking going national with franchises all over the country. She loved the idea and I was booked for television fame the third week of January.

Chapter Twenty-Six

S ounds like a fairytale, doesn't it? Old lady wins lots of money and starts a business that becomes uber successful after almost being arrested for basically running a brothel out of her home.

Well, it's true. Molly's Matchmaking got a Shark and an infusion of one hundred thousand dollars to expand the business. The television pitch was done by me, Jake (who became our financial genius) and all three roommates who posed with handsome seventy something clients.

From four mahjongg playing old ladies to four woman who now drove fancy cars, we no longer had to sell our own kisses and hugs.

Our lives had changed.

Peta and Bernie: They bought a house around the corner from me. Peta also is starring in Silver Lake's Senior Follies which will open in April. Bernie is back doing a little modeling on weekends when she isn't interviewing prospective clients.

Sophie: She's engaged to Joe and moved in with him a few weeks ago and credits her finding love again to our club.

Me: I'm up to my elbows busy with the Matchmaking business. We look to be franchised in at least ten cities by next year. Jake rented his house and moved in with me. We couldn't be happier. My son Stanley, you know, the lawyer, is relieved the club is no more and actually said he is proud of me. Why shouldn't he be? After all, he now will have a whopping inheritance.

Finally, after seventy-three years, I've become a success in my own rights.

Finally, it's Molly's turn.

Acknowledgements

Kathy Strong - You've been cheering me on from the start. Thanks, dear friend.

Emily Perl Kingsley – You're my dictionary and my dear friend for over fifty years. I love and admire you.

Dr. Dale Atkins – I think you're my lucky charm. To get a positive review from such an esteemed author and brilliant woman is amazing. Thank you!

Super thanks to John Asher and Jordan Reid. Let's get this done!!!

Thanks to my family – Jonathan, Julia, Justin, Nga, Khai, Milo and Rachel. Again, I'm <u>NOT</u> Mistress Molly.

Dr. Lily Rich – you never stop encouraging me. A huge thank you.

And lastly – to all my buddies in Hippyville, thank you for letting me pick your brains and laughing along with me.

Other books by Sherry Halperin available on Amazon.com or by contacting the author:

sherryhalperin@aol.com

Rescue Me, He's Wearing A Moose Hat
and 40 Other Dates After 50

Reviews: "*Rescue Me* is funny, realistic, and inspiring. It's the perfect companion for any woman over fifty who's reentering the dating world. Its brief, vivid chapters provide food for thought about life, love, and self-knowledge for all woman, married or single, of any age." Nancy Thayer, author of The Hot Flash Club series.

"Rescue Me reads like a thriller. It's funny, poignant, horrifying, and inspirational, with the perfect – and perfectly unexpected – happy ending." Harley Jane Kozak, Agatha Award winning author of Dating Dead Men and Dating Is Murder

Just Call Me Lady – A Romantic Comedy

"What a delightful read! Sherry Halperin's heroine exuberantly seizes a chance at experiencing the glamourous life of royalty and discovers, braving innumerable obstacles and challenges, the veracity of the adage "be careful what you wish for." This adventurous and humorous escapade subtly guides our heroine through a captivating journey of self-exploration, evaluation of life values and the real meaning of love. Great fun.

Emily Perl Kingsley, Former Sesame Street writer and multiple Emmy Award winner

"Author Sherry Halperin takes her heroine on an adventure that is only a fantasy to most of us. An Eliza Doolittle transformation, royal titles, elbowing with the rich and famous and European travels all play a part in Connie's journey of self-discovery. It's a Hallmark movie just waiting to be made!!"

Kathy

"The characters were so genuine and funny. Just seem to know them. Love Constance. Such an enjoyable book to read." Deborah

"Sherry Halperin has written a hilarious escape comedy about love and how to find it. What could be a better setting than an art gallery in the desert, a fantasy make-over and European escapades? I loved following the heroine on her journey. The writing is very conversational and I felt like I was listening to my best friend talking about her life! I couldn't put it down. Should be a movie! Just what we all need now."

Joy

About The Author

Sherry Halperin was born and raised in Beacon, New York. As a teen, she studied at the Dramatic Workshop in New York City and spent five summers at Cecilwood Theatre in Fishkill, New York as a summer stock apprentice alongside such notables as Barbra Streisand, Dustin Hoffman and Peter Fonda. She went West for College and received her degree from the Pasadena Playhouse College of Fine Arts with a major in directing.

Ms. Halperin has consistently worked on projects in the arts from distributing feature films, agenting actors, directing stage productions and working on hundreds of hours of network and cable television as a writer, producer and director. She was a producer on the award-winning feature film Adopt A Sailor and was honored to be a past president of Women In Film and Television.

Her books, Recue Me, He's Wearing A Moose Hat, Just Call Me Lady and now, Mistress Molly have all been optioned for possible films.

Sherry is a humorist who strongly believes in the power of laughter to heal, enhance and empower a fulfilling life.

She resides in Santa Cruz, California with her six-pound poodle, Clouseau, loves playing Ukulele on the beach, has two great sons, two beautiful daughters-in-laws and two fabulous grandsons.